THE BROKEN BUSH

JAMIE SCOTT

The Broken Bush
Jamie Scott

1st Edition © 2013
2nd Edition © 2021

For my Family

SYNOPSIS: -

Angus McLean and his new wife leave the Scottish Highlands and get propelled from an idyllic dream to epic nightmare when the Rhodesian bush war intensifies. Returning
from a bush patrol at the wildlife station, Angus and his team
is devastated when the terrorists strike.

Refusing to leave his post at the station, along with the
rest of his team, they do what they do best tracking though
the African bush. But now the quarry is human as their
humanitarian efforts turn to hunting down insurgents.

As the war effort deepens, the wildlife station has regular
contact with various units of the Rhodesian military gaining
the art of war from their experiences.

An untimely death brings a new Dutch female vet to the
station, Annika Vandekamp. Annika is beautiful and forth-
right, and their budding relationship forces Angus to face
some of his more sheltered experiences of his life.

CHAPTER 1

*T*wo long wheelbase Land Rover Safaris, both with two rows of seats in the rear, followed by an Isuzu caged back truck, raised a cloud of red dust. The convoy bumped its way along the dirt road he through the Rhodesian bush. They were headed for the primary base of the area station for the department of game and wildlife, In the Nyanga district of Manicaland fifty kilometres short of the Mozambique border.

Driving the leading Land Rover was Angus McLean, head game warden. The wiry Scotsman locked his sweat soaked muscles tense as he fought with the steering wheel to keep the vehicle steady on the rough track. His eyes stung with the sweat as it flowed from the brim of his bush hat.

Beside him sat Lindani, his Shona tracker, a powerfully built man, as tall as him but more muscular, his shaved head looked like a glistening ebony carving.

Lindani had grown up here and had learned his craft from his father, who had been a tracker at the station when it had been a hunting lodge. For the previous three years since he'd come to Rhodesia, he had been a mentor to Angus, showing him the ways of the African bush and teaching him the Shona language. Lindani was not only a co-worker but a good friend, as were their wives.

Angus had grown up in Wester Ross on the rugged North West coast of Scotland where he lived with his parents and older sister. His father was head gamekeeper and Ghillie to the Bad Na Baighe Estate.

The hundred-thousand-acre estate, had been in the hands of the Donaldson-McMaster family for four generations; a family who had made their fortunes in the colonies of the Empire with tea from their plantations in India, rubber from Malaysia and tobacco from the Americas, but their wealth had changed as the colonies gained independence.

The current laird Bruce Donaldson was struggling to keep the estate intact as it supported the livelihoods of many of its farming tenants, mainly livestock farmers of sheep and a few small dairy herds.

But its primary income came from the wealthy clients who came to enjoy the outdoor pursuits it offered such as red deer stalking on the higher ground, grouse shooting on the moorland, salmon fishing in the river Laxford. It also offered trout fishing in the many small lochs, and pheasant shooting in the thick pine woods.

Angus's mother was a housekeeper at the Lairds Victorian granite-built house. Home for his family was a little traditional crofter's cottage tied to the estate, where both he and his sister had been born in one of the two bedrooms upstairs.

Leaving school two months after his fifteenth birthday, Angus had assisted his father on shoot days working either as a beater or gun bearer and various other odd jobs around the estate. He was accomplished, both with a rod and gun, having shot his first stag when he was twelve.

The Laird had called for him on his seventeenth birthday

and asked if he had been willing to sponsor him would he take a course at Aberdeen University for a degree in land management.

Three years later he returned, taking up the position of estate manager. His duties had included arranging shoot days, making sure there were sufficient beaters. Those people were made up of local farmhands and crofters.

As the locals arrived at a shoot one Saturday morning on the back of the tractor trailer, a girl climbed down with the men. She wasn't dressed for a shoot; she wore blue jeans and a wax jacket, a green roll-neck sweater and square-toed boots on her feet. Her raven black hair highlighted her pale skin, which complimented her ice-blue eyes, and he noted it was his sister's friend since her school days, Morag McLeod.

Although two years older than him, he'd admired her beauty from a distance in his youth. Bravely, he'd asked her to dance at a ceilidh the year he'd left school, but she'd just laughed at him. Morag did not accompany the shoot but was she greeted by his sister Jean but turned and looked back at him smiling as Morag and his sister took the lane to his parent's croft.

During supper that night, his sister, and Morag were seated across the table from him. As they whispered and giggled, he felt his face redden, knowing he was the subject of their amusement.

Morag slept in his sister's room that night and walked with them to church the next day. When the service was over, she went home with her parents in their green Morris Minor. Her parents had a small croft four miles away where her father raised sheep. It wasn't a large croft house and similar to his, except they had a barn where her father would house his flock during the worst of the vicious winter snows.

While Angus sat in his room reading that night his sister knocked the door and came in, they were closer than they had been when they were younger. Jean told him Morag had been going on about him, how he matured and was very handsome. His face flushed.

"She really fancies you Angus don't shy away from her," she'd advised.

Six months later they got married at the church with both families and the laird and his wife in attendance. The laird had arranged for all the wedding guests to attend the post wedding celebrations in the main hall of his manor.

A year later, their first wedding anniversary was not a day for celebration; the laird had called all the staff the day before. He told them because of his financial position he was being forced to break up the estate; the sale was subject to contracts being exchanged. He told them the new owners were a middle eastern consortium, but he was not aware of their plans.

As Laird's family retained the house and formal gardens, they kept his father on as handyman, but there was no job for Angus. Following this, he tried other work but could not settle to farm labouring, which was the only work the area offered because the new owners had no immediate plans for the estate.

Three months after the Laird's announcement, Angus had been sitting at breakfast when noticed a little advertisement in the national newspaper looking for a game warden with the Rhodesian Wildlife department. A little coupon attached at the bottom of the ad asking for basic information such as name, address, and age. As this was all it had asked for, Angus filled it in and sent it off to an address in London.

Two weeks had passed when he'd received a letter inviting him to attend an interview in Edinburgh. He travelled there with Morag; it was the first time they had been to a big city together. He told the interviewees all about himself and produced his university degree. When the interview was over, they spent the rest of the day touring the city before catching an evening train north again.

Three weeks passed when the offer of the job came, and eight weeks later he and Morag left amidst tears and hugs from both their families as they said their goodbyes on the platform of the single-track railway station.

CHAPTER 2

*A*ngus and his tracker, Lindani had cut short their planned three-day bush patrol anxious they could not make radio contact with the base all day. The sets in the vehicles could communicate with each other so they knew the problem was not with their radios, and they also knew the chance of the two set at the station being out of order at the same time was remote.

They made their way up the top of a rise on the plateau where the high savannah dropped away to the lush Nyanga valley below. Lindani touched his forearm on the steering wheel and pointed to the sky. In the distance he could just make out the black spots circling against the cloudless blue sky. Angus braked and brought up his binoculars to his eyes, confirming his first thoughts. The vultures where over the region of the station.

He slipped the gear leaver in to first and edge forward at a crawl before eventually stopping short of the ridge line and waited until the other two vehicles drew up behind his. Signalling them to wait, he took off and ran until he reached the top of the ridge.

He crept forward through the bush until he could see the valley stretch out before him. Using his binoculars again, he picked out the camp and zoomed the lenses to maximum strength. Nothing moved within the compound.

When he scanned the main building, there was still no movement. Angus continued to study the rest of the compound, where the animals in the holding pens and the windmill for the well were the only signs of movement. Seeing the workshops with the doors closed appeared unusual as we always left them open to avoid the unbearable heat when the sun shone on the corrugated roof and then he noticed the main gates were open.

"What is it, Angoos?" Angus was already tense but was startled by the whispered voice over his shoulder. Lindani's deep, rich Shona accent made his name sound like some cartoon character in a Walt Disney film.

Without breaking his focus through the binoculars, he said, "Something's not right."

"Gehena," his tracker muttered. Gehana was the Shona word for hell.

They made their way back through the bush to the vehicles and called the rest of the group to meet him. The five men gathered around them, the two flushers and the two assistant wardens. McLean did not trust his command of the Shona language; they could all speak English to varying degrees, except for Chatambuza which in Shona means troublesome.

Speaking in English, Angus explained the suspicious situation, then had Lindani repeat it in his native Shona. He ordered them to get their weapons and ammunition from the vehicles; he grabbed his Weatherbey .460 rifle from the gun rack and put the sling over his shoulder.

Lindani took down his Mauser 66SM .308 and did likewise. They made their way to the rear of the Land Rover and opened the gun case bolted to the back and took out the two matt black South Africa R1 7.62 carbines. Giving the thirty round magazines a light tap on the tailgate to ensure the rounds would not jam and rammed the home in the weapons, and into their breast pockets of their shirts, he called the men to gather round again.

"Chatambuza you and Dzingia take a Land Rover and go to Nyangia village first, tell the constable we have a problem at the station, and ask if he could send some officers, then head for the Matazari station.

Nyangia was a village with a population of around seven hundred people, the single main street had two stores and a police station manned by four police officers, and it had telephone land line.

"Then contact Mr Louie when you get in radio range and ask him if he can come with some of his men." Louie was Louie De-Langa a big South African he had worked at the Kruger national park before moving north with his wife Hette to join the Rhodesian game and wildlife service as head warden.

As they set off in the truck, Angus turned to the rest of the group. "Check all of your weapons are fully loaded." As they did so he added, "Mandala you stay here with the Land Rover and truck get them off the track… and make sure you have your radio switched on. when the constables get here follow them down to the station." Mandala nodded. Angus turned to the others. "The rest of you come with me. We're going to approach the station from the east where the bush is thickest and go into a buffalo flush formation."

They set off down the slope leading to the valley floor, moving to where the bush was thickest. Lindani took in the lead, and they spread out at ten paces apart in single file, as they would have on a buffalo flush, stopping every twenty paces to wait and listen. They had covered the space between them and the station with ease, but it felt had like an eternity.

When they approached the edge of the yellow sun-bleached elephant grass and halted, he pointed to the men to move in a flanking movement. Lindani broke off to his right Manodno to his left, and they moved forward in a straight line at the same ten meters apart.

, As they came to the edge of the grass, they stopped short of the open ground that separated them from the perimeter fence. Studying the area beyond the fence, still nothing moved. They had to cross the open ground exposed and without cover, there had been insurgency activity in Manica-land district but never in the Nyanga region.

From his position, Angus could see the front of the old south facing colonial building built on a slope, its white weather faded exterior topped by a green corrugated roof and steps leading up to the shaded stoep. The place was deserted and the main door to the building was closed; it was only ever closed at night. they always left it open during the day to allow what breezes if any to circulate its interior.

He scanned to the right towards the workshop, around a dozen black vultures roosted on the roof, hopping from one leg to the other as the hot tin burned their feet. As they emerged from the elephant grass, the vultures took to the air with lumbering wing beats to overcome the weight of their bulky bodies.

CHAPTER 3

*T*hey reached the wire perimeter fence built to keep animals out. The four bottom strands of wire had an electric current passing through them and skirted around it to where the main gates lay open.

When they reached it, he signalled to Lindani to go to the left and head for the side of the main building, and Manodno to go towards the holding pens, and approach the building from the back, they walked slowly over the red bare earth, weapons at the ready safety off fully alert eyes darting in every direction.

Reaching the ten steps leading up to the stoep and front door, he climbed the steps slowly with each wooden step creaking under his feet. When he reached the stoep, he paused for a moment in silence.

Lindani had slid over the stoep rail and came from his right. He reached for the door handle and turned it slowly with his left hand and turned it to open it. His hand flew back on the R1 fore stock, his other hand on the pistol grip with his finger poised just above the trigger. Using the muzzle of the weapon he pushed the door open slowly.

Daylight spilled in from the open door into the darkness of the hallway, and the scene looked chaotic. The hall tables were upturned, and the polished wooden floor and rug was littered with earth and broken earthenware of the plant pots.

The other doors of the hallway stood silently closed. Adrenaline rushed through Angus, and his breathing sounded ragged, his pulse raced, and it felt like his heart would explode. Angus's head ached, and he was drowning in sweat.

The doors to the left and right led to their accommodation suites, each containing a lounge, bedroom, and bathroom. The door at the far end of the hall led to the communal kitchen and dining room, used only in winter. The rest of the time they ate on the big table on the stoep.

He left the first door on the right as this was the station office and reached for the handle of the door to the left, the suite he shared with his wife Morag.

Lindani lifted the carbine to the ready position on his shoulder, Angus turned the door handle and pushed the door slowly open with the muzzle. Inside they found the same chaotic mess as the hall, with furniture knocked over, their personal possessions and clothes scattered, and a black comms radio lay smashed on the floor.

Quickly they moved through the lounge and Angus threw open the bedroom door; again, it was the same shambles. Next, they moved down the hallway to the suite Lindani shared with his wife Mazvita, with Lindani taking the lead this time, so, everything was destroyed and scattered.

They moved through the building quicker now, separating to speed up the search. There was no sign of life anywhere. They headed to the kitchen, opened the door, and found it empty with wrecked pots and pans, crockery smashed as flour and coffee covered the floor. They jumped as they heard the voice.

Manodno spoke from the other side of the fly screen door. "I come in now, yes?"

McLean shouted, "Spread out, search the whole compound." He looked at Lindani. "You take the vets building I'll take the workshops." Instead of moving slowly and stealthily, they raced across the red open ground together.

Lindani broke off to the left towards the building where the vet Willie Bekker treated any sick or wounded animals, they brought in. Willie was an old Afrikaner; a little thin man with a dour face that never seemed to smile or show any emotion, and his white pancho-villa style moustache added to his dourness.

As Lindani neared the workshop, he slowed as he approached the last few feet. Staring at the big wooden doors, he reached to open them and stopped dead in his tracks when he heard the buzz of flies.

Instantly, his heart felt as if it was pumping molasses though his veins, and the sweet sickly smell of death and blood filled his nostrils. He yanked the big door open with such force it crashed hard against the front of the workshop, sending a mist fine red dust that had built up over the years falling from the rafters.

His eyes squinted as they adjusted towards the gloom, where a big cloud of blue shining blow flies mingled with the showering red dust as they swarmed out from the building.

Lindani retched but nothing came up he felt his heart squeeze, he thought he was chocking bulging veins stretched on his temples. Manodno dropped his weapon and fell to his knees as he glared at the horror the building held inside.

Everyone at the station had been massacred. They had all been slaughtered, their blood had darkening the earthen floor of the workshop. Their bodies had been heaped on top of each other where they had been hacked to death. The stench from the afternoon sun on the tin roof had made it into an oven.

Angus strode over to where both men stood in shock before the big doors. "What is it? What's happened?" he asked. When he saw the carnage inside his jaw dropped and froze there. The whites of Lindani's eyes looked stark in shock against his ebony face as tears started to run down his black dust covered cheeks. They had lost track of time, it had stopped, and nobody spoke a word as they stood or knelt in a trance like state as the shadows grew longer.

a noise suddenly snapped them out of the nightmare were sharing. When two French built Alouette helicopters came screaming low over the station, circled the scene and landed obscured by a cloud of red dust just inside the main gates. Eight uniformed bodies jumped from the aircraft before they had touched down.

They spread out, running their rifles at the ready, the one at the front issuing orders. Two men took up positions between the helicopters and the gates, the others headed in their direction. It took McLean a few seconds to register the voice it had felt out of place to hear "Military" in the dusty heat and with the smell of death hanging heavy in the air.

"How long ago did this happen?" The voice was Scottish, not like Angus's highland lilt but rougher a west coast accent, a Glasgow accent, which had sounded incongruent in the bush.

Got it, he thought. This is only a dream, no not a dream, a fucking nightmare.

The clatter of blades came from a third helicopter circling

the station but didn't seem to have any intention of landing Angus stood watching it and it brought him back to reality.

He realised the Glaswegian's voice was talking to him. "When did this happen?" but all Angus could do was shrug his shoulders and stare at him "You're the warden here, right?" Angus nodded. "Let's get you all away from here, eh?" he said, in a softer tone. "Come on" but the Glasgow accent made it sounded like "comoan."

Angus watched as the Glaswegian lifted his radio. "Same as before," he said into it. A distant tinny voice came back at him. "You lot stay there tonight, make the place secure, support will arrive in the morning."

Immediately after the communication, both grounded helicopters wound up their engines, shrouding the area in a dust cloud again. The two soldiers who had been securing the gate ran over to the machines and came running away with two big rucksacks over their shoulders, their FN rifles in one hand a machine gun in the other.

The air support took off in a cloud of red dust and had vanished over a tall ridge less than minute later. Silence returned, suddenly the Glaswegian's voice punctured the quiet.

"There's only the three of you, right?"

"No," Angus answered, still in a trancelike state. "Six."

The soldier frowned. "But I only count three?"

"Shit," Angus replied, "I forgot about Mandala." He reached for his radio and hit the transmit button. "Mandala come in." he ordered.

"Yes, Angoos, I'm here. No constables have come. What do you want me to do?"

Angus clicked the transmit button on his radio again. "Make sure there are no weapons in the Land Rover and drive it off the road. Bring the keys and come down with truck to the station, understand?"

"Yes," Mandala replied.

"Out," Angus said and lowered his radio. He glanced back at the soldier. "I forgot we left him with the transport."

The soldier held out his hand. "My name is Ewan… Sandy Ewan."

Angus reached out and took his hand "Angus McLean."

"We've got support people coming in the morning," he informed Angus in case he'd missed that fact.

Angus nodded. "But what about…" he stopped talking and nodded towards the workshops.

"Best leave it tonight. You've all had enough for one day, eh?"

He put a hand on his shoulder. "Let's get you all up there." He nodded in the direction of the main building.

They arrived on the big "L" shaped stoep that ran the full length of the building and along the left had side.

"Take Kiwi, take Jacko with you and secure that gate for the night. Stick a claymore to one side," Ewan said to one of his men.

"What about Mandala," Angus asked.

"What's he driving?"

"An open top truck," Angus replied.

"Secure the gates and wait it out until the truck comes and get him in."

"Okay, boss," came the reply in a thick New Zealand accent.

Ewan turned to his other five men. "Right, get busy the rest of you. One gimpy on the front of the porch, the other at the side, Claymores blind side of the veranda and back."

Angus and his men just stood in silence on the stoep as if afraid to enter the building, watching the soldiers go about their business. Each gimpy or FN MAG 7.62 general purpose machine gun had a tripod which unfolded from the front end of the barrel and placed into position. He watched the soldier nearest to them as he set gun up on its tripod.

"Stop a feckin train these will," in informed them in a heavy Irish brogue.

When the soldiers had secured the surroundings, Angus and his men sat in silence around the big table on the stoep and watched another soldier close the door of the workshop. It was almost dark twilight, which is a very brief affair in Rhodesia, the sun vanishing beneath the horizon as quick as it rises at dawn.

As Ewan climbed the steps at the front of the stoep, he looked towards Angus where he sat on a bench at the table, his head hung on his chest.

"Just thought I'd have someone close the doors," he informed him in a quiet voice.

Angus stood up, walked over, and sat beside him. "Thanks."

"How did you come to be here?" Ewan asked.

As Angus told him his story, Ewan noticed him finger a stag horn protruding from the top of his calf length bush boot. When he mentioned his wife, his eyes welled until eventually tears spilled down his cheeks. He sobbed, his hand covering his eyes. A few moments later, he wiped the tears from his eyes and cheeks and glanced back at Ewan.

Ewan nodded to his boot. "What's that?"

Angus gripped the horn and drew out the one-hundred-and-twenty-millimetre double-edged blade. "It's my Sgàin-Dubh." He looked back to Ewan. "What about you, how did you get to be here?"

"Same sort of thing served my time as a marine engineer working in the shipyards. Orders dried up, got a job in a mine in the south of the country in a place called Shabani. Sold the house back home came here bought a house, the mine was mothballed because of terrorist attacks and there was no other work to be had anywhere. So, I sent my wife to live with her sister in South Africa we don't have enough money to go home, so here I am."

Angus stood up again. "I think I'll start the main generator and get some lights on." As he turned to go, Ewan touched his forearm.

"It might be better if we didn't tonight, so as not to attract unwanted attention, eh?" as he said this, he suddenly heard the noise of an engine humming in the distance. It wasn't Mandala coming back, he had come back half an hour before.

"Can you hear an engine somewhere?" he asked.

Angus informed him it was the small generator that ran the fridges, freezers, and water pump. "It cuts out automatically when the main generator starts and kicks in when it's shut down."

"What do you guys do here? The other guys, I mean."

"The stocky one is Lindani, he's the tracker, and he's been here all his life. People talk about having a sixth sense Lindani has one and more, he can see things you don't think are there. They call him Shavi in Shona, it means spirit. That guy moves through the bush with no sound or trace. He's been trying to teach me how, but I don't imagine I'll get to his level in this life. Mandala and Manodno are my assistant wardens. There's another two, Dzingia and Chatambuza. They're the flushers, but I sent them to Matazari to get help."

"Can I ask you a question?" said Angus

"Fire away," Ewan replied.

"How long did it take you to get here today? I thought your nearest base was fifty miles north of Nyanga."

Ewan eyed him, cautiously. "We were on another job."

"Where?" Angus probed.

Ewan hesitated before he replied. "Matazari station, that's where your other two guys found us."

"Is that what you meant when you told the voice on the radio? What happened over there?" Angus asked, nodding towards Matazari.

"Same as happened here, except they raised that place to the ground." Angus paused for a moment.

"What about De-Langa?"

"Don't know there was only one white body, a woman."

"Christ Hette?"

"Listen, you'll have to get some sleep," Ewan advised.

"HOW THE HELL CAN I SLEEP?" Angus shrieked and stormed off into the building. He went to the kitchen and found Lindani sitting at the table, head down crying, shoulders shaking. He glanced up when he'd heard Angus, tears running down his cheeks. Angus said nothing to him and put a hand on his broad shoulder. The touch broke him and they both wept openly.

"Fuck it," Angus said after a few minutes and went to the chest in the pantry. He came back with a bottle of Cape brandy and two enamel mugs. He poured and shoved a mug toward his tracker. "Here get this down you, there's no way we'll sleep tonight."

Drowning their sorrows, they both drank like they had come out of the desert. Two bottles later they were both slumped on the table.

CHAPTER 5

*A*ngus and Lindani woke with a start. It was daylight, and the air became filled with the clattering sound of helicopter engines again. Both men's eyes looked puffy and swollen. Stumbling to their feet, they made their way to the stoep; the daylight stabbing their eyes.

"Support unit" said Ewan informed them, nodding to where they'd landed as eight more troops climbed out of the two Alouettes with backpacks and rifles. Ewan turned to Angus. "They'll want all of you to stay here in the building while they clear up the workshop."

Angus shook his head. "I'm coming with you."

Ewan held up a hand in protest. "No, you're not. They need to do it alone. These fuckers might have booby trapped the place. These guys know what they're doing," he insisted, nodding in the direction of the new arrivals.

Angus and Lindani watched in silence as the support unit headed for the workshop with their bundles on their backs, noting the doors had been opened sometime earlier to dissipate the heat.

No one spoke as they sat quietly waiting until fifteen

minutes later when they exited the workshop and came over to the main building. Ewan walked over to meet one of the soldiers before he turned and came over to where Angus's men stood. He shook his head, a grim expression on his face.

"It's not good news. Eight bodies, two women and six men."

Angus and Lindani were immediately overcome with grief. Their bodies shook, shocked again by what they already suspected had happened.

"My wife, I want to see my wife," Angus screamed as he tried to leave the stoep. Ewan gripped his arm and the soldier who had come to the stoep placed a hand on his chest.

"Better if you didn't. They've been cut up badly. We've already placed them in the body bags." Angus stood shaking and sobbing with Ewan still holding his arm, shaking his head in sympathy.

Mandala came out with one of the enamel mugs and handed it to Angus. "Here, drink this."

He threw back the brandy, and it burned his throat. Immediately he wretched pushed Ewan out of his way and leaned over the stoep rail where he threw up. He hadn't eaten the night before and all that came up was the previous night's brandy, the liquid splashing as it hit the red earth. When his body finally stopped convulsing, he straightened up, drawing the palm of his hand across his mouth. His vision was blurred as tears streamed from his eyes from the effects of being sick and from grief.

Mandala appeared beside him again. "Coffee."

Angus took the mug and walked to the table where he saw Lindani slumped over it, his head in his broad folded forearms, his body convulsing with grief. He slid into the seat next to him and touched his elbow. Lindani looked up, then threw his arms round Angus's neck. Returning the hug, they both joined in their grief, both men weeping openly. Giving them privacy, the others left the stoep in silence.

The six freshly dug graves at the rear of the house were dug in the shade of the Acacia tree with a body bag lying next to each one. Inside, Ewan approached Angus and Lindani as they lay in the semi darkness of the room, Lindani on a sofa, Angus slumped on a big armchair. The medic with the support team had given them a sedative injection he to calm them.

Ewan touched Angus's arm, and he woke with a start. "You needed to sleep."

Noting their shadows were long as he stood up, he looked through the sun filter nets on the window. "What time is it? Last thing I remember I was sitting on the stoep," Angus muttered. As he spoke, Lindani let out a groan as he stirred.

"Quarter to five," Ewan said.

As both men became fully awake, Mandala entered the room with two enamel mugs. "Drink, it's chicken soup."

As they sat in silence sipping the soup, Ewan cleared his throat. "I hate to say this, but we need to bury the bodies."

Angus shook his head, no. "I want to see my wife."

Ewan grimaced. "Better not, Angus. The lads said the bodies are badly mutilated."

"It doesn't matter, I want to see her," he insisted.

"I also what to see my wife," Lindani insisted, nodding in agreement.

Ewan shrugged and sighed. "Well, if you are both sure I can't stop you."

As all three men walked through the back door, they froze when they saw the freshly dug graves. Tears immediately streamed down both men's cheeks. As they approached the graves, one of the support team stood guard.

"Which one is Mrs McLean?" Ewan asked the soldier. He

indicated to the last body bag in the row. "And Lindani which one is his wife?" The guard pointed to another.

Both men stood staring at the black shiny bags.

"Do you want us here? Ewan asked.

"Leave us if you don't mind," Angus replied.

As Ewan walked away, both he and Lindani knelt beside the bags. Angus reached out and let his fingers gently touch the waterproof material, stroking it. His hand moved towards the top where he paused, and sob tore from his throat.

Reaching for the metal zipper, he slowly slid it down, stopping about eighteen inches from where he'd started. Letting go, he folded back the material with his eyes closed. Swallowing hard, he slowly opened his eyes again and stared at what used to be his wife. His breath caught in his throat. Morag's head looked bruised almost beyond recognition, eyes purple and closed. Dried blood coated her face.

His hand touched her blood matted hair. "Jesus Christ, Morag, what have I done? I should never have brought you to this place. We should have stayed in Scotland." he bent and kissed her swollen lips. "Goodbye darling," he whispered as he slowly closed the zip. He rose from the bag, turned, and walked towards the back door. Once inside, he nodded to Ewan and the others.

"Would you like me to conduct a service for your wife?" Another of the soldiers asked him.

Angus stared at him, a soldier asking to conduct a funeral service. He noticed the little brass crosses on each collar of his shirt and nodded.

Going back outside, they all gathered around the graves as the Chaplin conducted the service while the others stood in silence. Angus only realised it had ended when he heard the words "Ashes to ashes, dust to dust." He bowed his head throughout as the bodies were being lowered into the ground.

He went to Lindani, put an arm around his shoulder and led him back to the back door. With their work done, the other support unit had taken off shortly after the funeral and the mood in the building felt solemn that night.

CHAPTER 6

They all sat on the stoep that night the moon was high and bathed the compound in its blue light a small breeze was stirring the trees Angus and his men were starting to get worse for wear with the brandy.

"Come on," Angus said to Ewan, "have a drink for Christ's sake, man. You can't go to a funeral without a drink."

Ewan studied Angus for a moment then turned to the rest of his men "Okay," he said, directing his attention to them. "three beers each and no more." They all sat in the stoep's shadow and a few conversations started between them.

"Hyenas," Lindani suddenly said, and silence fell among the men as they listened.

"I can't hear anything except for the trees rustling and the crickets," Ewan murmured after a few moments.

"If he says they're there, they must be close by," Angus told him. They sat again in silence.

Then they heard the giggling and whooping, "Told you, Lindani's senses are way beyond ours." He turned his gaze back to Ewan. "Which grave is Willie Bekker in?"

Ewan looked puzzled. "Who is Willie Bekker?"

"He was the vet. His was here but he covered the Matazari area as well."

Ewan screwed his eyes up in thought. "A white man?" Angus nodded. "Hm, it was all black males in the graves."

The hyenas sounded closer and more excited "They're down behind the skinning station by the generator," Lindani announced. They want to feed off something there.

Angus leapt to his feet, grabbed his R1 and took off running towards the skinning shed. Ewan in his wake. The station's two ridgeback dogs overtook them both and rounded to the back of the shed. Their barking joined in with the din of the hyenas. As he opened the skinning station door, the bright moonlight spilled inside and Willie's naked body hung on the skinning rack, his feet tied with rope and hung on a hook. He looked like a ghost in the moonlight, his once grey moustache appearing like a big red smile on his face. The man was stripped and beaten to death; his ghostly body covered in purple welt marks.

The hyenas were at fever pitch by then on the other side of the fence. Angus let off two shots in the air and they sulked away into the bush. The shots brought the rest on Ewan's troop running in their direction.

"False alarm Jacko you and Kiwi down here the rest back to the veranda," Ewan ordered. Angus caught the Glaswegian term he'd used. Everybody else called it the stoep here. It was the second time he had heard him use it.

Jacko and Kiwi arrived.

"What's up boss?" Jacko asked when he and Kiwi arrived.

Ewan nodded towards the shed. "Cut him down."

Angus spoke into his radio. "Mandala, bring some blankets over here."

"Copy," Mandala replied. When he arrived, they wrapped

Willie's body and carried back to rear of the building. They buried him in the moonlight, but without a sermon, as the Chaplain had left already.

When they returned to the stoep, Ewan sat next to Angus on the steps.

"We need to leave in the morning. The choppers are coming at first light. What are your plans now?

Angus frowned. "Stay here, what else? I have a score to settle with these fuckers and this is my home."

Ewan shook his head. "Don't be stupid. Other guys in your situation have had the same idea— most of them ended up dead."

Angus shrugged his shoulders. "It's better if you leave — us to do that work."

"Well, if that's what you want, why not sign up?" Ewan asked.

He thought about the proposition for a few seconds. "Nah," he replied, got up and walked into his room.

Next morning, they were all up and about as the dawn crept in. Mandala had laid the table on the stoep with sliced ham, boiled eggs, pancakes, and coffee. There had been an unusually' light shower of rain during the night and the morning smelled fresh, a cocktail of wet earth and vegetation.

"Are you sure you and your men want to stay here?" Ewan asked. Angus didn't answer, just nodded. "My advice if you're determined to stay is to put some defensive measures in place. As this is the first time the insurgents have come this far in from the border, it won't be the last.

"We're quite well armed and if they come back, it won't be so easy as it was with station hands and our women."

"You need to prepare for a mass attack," Ewan told him. He turned to Jacko. "Bring the H.E. bag." Jacko did as he asked, and Ewan placed it on the table. Carefully lifting the contents out of the bag, he glanced toward Angus again. "This is H.E.—high explosives," he clarified, as he placed the oblong grease proof block on the table.

Beside it he placed metallic pencil like objects next to the block. He nodded towards the far corner of the station next to the workshop where unwanted bits and pieces had accumulated over the years. "See those oil drums? I want you to cut the lids, not right off, just enough that it acts like a hinge. Taking out his knife, Ewan cut a one inch, slice from the HE block of explosive. Picking up one of the pencil objects, he inserted it into the putty-like explosive. Attach a long wire to these two, put it in the bottom of an oil drum and dump any crap you have lying around in there was well. You could use that mountain of beer bottles over there, and you'll have a personal mine. Another thing to do for added effect is pour shit in it so when you set it off. Those of them it doesn't kill who has cuts, they'll get infected by the shit."

After he'd giving his instruction, Ewan and his troop packed up all their kits. A short time later they all sat on the stoep together.

"The helicopters are coming now," Linlani told them.

"Soon," Ewan agreed.

"No, they come now," the tracker insisted.

A few seconds later Ewan heard the distant familiar clatter of the blades.

He looked at Angus with a raised eyebrow.

"See what I mean?" Angus asked with a shrugged and threw Ewan a wink.

As the men shook hands, Angus had one more request. "Would you have these posted when you get back to the barracks?" He handed Ewan two blue air mail envelopes he had written while it was still dark in his room. "They are to Morag's and my parents, telling them what has happened?"

Ewan gave a sympathetic nodded. "Sure."

Angus shook hands with the other soldiers.

"We will let the game department what's gone on here," Ewan told him as he left Angus and joined the rest of his men.

CHAPTER 7

$\mathcal{T}$he sound of the helicopters faded into the distance, and they all sat in silence.

"Are you going back to your village," Angus asked his tracker.

"No, I come with you find the people who did this terrible thing and kill them, yes?"

Angus nodded, "Yes." he turned to the others. "You can go to your homes now."

"No, Angoos. We come too they come make my friends sad and kill others," Mandala explained. The others nodded their agreement.

"Okay," he agreed, and Mandala's face broke into a big white toothy smile. "Right, let's get things sorted out here. Lindani what animals are in Mr Willie's hospital?"

"Only a few. A cheetah with an inflamed paw, a zebra that had the lump cut from its neck and three impalas," he said.

"Is the cheetah still lame?" Lindani he shook his head. "Turn him loose. What about the zebra? When Lindani told him it only had stitches in the wound Angus said, "That can go as well and move the impala in to the holding pens."

Lindani set off about his task Angus turned to the others.

"Manodno, you go to the big house and throw out what's broken and put everything else back to how it was, Mandala you come with me. We'll remove the earth from the work-shop floor."

When Lindani was free, he went to him in the workshop; the Isuzu was backed up and they piled the rear high with red soil on top of a green tarpaulin.

"Do you want help, Angoos?" he shook his head. "No Lindani, get the dogs from the kennels, feed them, then do a sweep five hundred meters from the perimeter fence. See, if you can pick the spoor of these bastards who did this."

When Lindani opened the kennel door, the dogs came running. The two big Rhodesian Ridgebacks were brothers, measuring seventy centimetres to the shoulder, their heads at waist height.

Excited tails swung wildly when they came and sat beside him. The tracker had raised them from pups six years before, and they knew his ways with no commands being given. It was as if they could read his thoughts. He set off with the dogs a few yards in front of him, noses to the ground, working slowly as he had taught them and vanished into the bush.

With the back on the Isuzu loaded with earth piled on top of a green tarpaulin; they had to remove the top seventy centimetres of the soil before they came to clean earth. Sweat ran down both Angus and Mandala's bodies, both streaked like red zebras with the red earth in the late morning heat, and the tinderbox conditions from the sun shining on the corrugated tin roof.

"Let's get out of here, Mandala," Angus said. They drove

the truck to the main gates and left it there, before heading back to the main building.

After they'd both showered, they joined Manodno on the stoep. On the table, food sat at the centre covered with a domed net. As they ate, Manodno appeared with a bottle of Castle lager in each hand.

"This will cool your inside, Angoos." He laid them on the table, the condensation from the chilled bottles ran onto the table. Picking it up, he took a long drink and felt the cold beer to his stomach as he removed the bottle from his lips.

"Take the truck out into the bush and unload that earth. Just tie the tarpaulin to something and drag it off the back, cut some green Elephant grass so we can smoke out the workshop and don't hang about," he instructed Mandala and Manodno.

"What supplies to we need? Manodno will you make up a list and you can go with Chatambuza to Nyanga when the others come back."

Shortly after noon the Land Rover drove down towards the station in a cloud of red dust and halted in front of the steps. Dzingia and Chatambuza climbed out of the vehicle, Manodno with them spoke in rapid Shona, and Angus knew what he'd told them when their faces became sullen and drawn.

"Go homes this isn't your fight" Dzingia shook his head, his face solemn.

"No Angoos we stay with you we're friends We find these people."

Angus studied him. "Are you sure?" He nodded. "You're mad Dzingia. You're all fucking mad... fucking Africa is mad." A big toothy grin split the two ebony faces.

After they had eaten, he went to the workshop and lit a fire in the centre of the freshly dug earth. When it was well alight, he threw the green foliage on it. As the smoke filled the building, he closed the doors.

"The smoke will kill off any blow fly eggs and maggots, just check it regularly and keep the fire going for the rest of the day. Now, let's see if we can do anything with the radios."

He laid them on the table and examined the two radios. They had smashed both. He didn't know how to fix them and spent the rest of the afternoon taking parts from one and fitting them into the other to make one that worked.

Lindani returned mid-afternoon and told him he'd found the spoor. The shower of rain the previous night had washed away all but a few signs, but the tracker had found them where no one else would have.

He assessed there were around fifteen in the party and felt they were not people who knew how to move in the bush unnoticed as they had stuck to game trails. They had been smoking, leaving cigarette ends in view, Lindani said they had come from the northeast and left by the southeast. He paused then told Angus there were tracks of fifteen from the northeast, but when he picked up the spoor on the southeast, he'd found something unusual there. It was the spoor of seventeen, two of which had bush skills, not with them but tracking the main group.

Angus asked if he knew who the followers were, and he nodded with a smile. "They have smooth soled boots they leave no pattern." Angus had met men wearing these boots before; and it took a few seconds to let the news sink in.

"Army issue boots?"

The smile turned to a grin on Lindani's face. "Chipoko uto" he said. "Selous Scouts, ghost soldiers." These were the terrorists' terrorist who struck fear into the insurgents, operating in two-man teams they lived off the land.

Tracking them as they came over the border and passing their locations on for the regular army units to set up ambush points. The Rhodesian Light Infantry; would para-chute men in and herd the ZANU and ZAPU terrorists into a kill zone.

This gave him the satisfaction something was being done. He turned his attention back to the task at hand; see if he could get a radio that worked out of the bits he had spread before him on the table.

When Angus thought it would work, he tried it; nothing so set about rearranging the parts and tried again. This time the dial lit up he shouted and punched the air he turned the tuning dial—nothing.

Lindani came into the room and asked if it was working. Angus told him the dial lit up, but he couldn't tune in to anything then he noticed he hadn't connected the antenna; he did so, and the room filled with static; he turned the dial and room filled with music.

"Can you hear the drums, Fernando?" it was Abba. He'd tuned in to RBC The Rhodesian Broadcasting Corporation. He and Lindani grinned at each other.

"Angoos has fixed the radio," Lindani shouted over and over after running out the door. They all crowded into the room wearing wide grins, their faces beaming.

"Take a handset outside and switch it on," he told Lindani as he did so. He tuned the dial to their frequency, lifted the microphone to his mouth and pressed the transmit button.

"Nygana station calling. Can you hear me?"

A reply came back, "Yes," and the others let out a cheer.

"We're getting there," Angus told them. "Now listen, we need to carry a weapon at all times." He had opened the gun safe in the basement below the stoep earlier and had taken out the other two R1 carbines they had on the station and issued them all with handguns.

After dinner they sat around the table. "We have to be on our guard at all times, keep the vehicles filled up with fuel and don't get complacent. We'll have two people on guard during darkness while the others take turns sleeping. Four hours on, four offs. Manodno you and Chatambuza take the first shift and tomorrow you both remain in the station get the old flour sacks from the workshop, fill them with earth and stack the round the stoep rail to make a wall." they both nodded. He told the rest of them to get some sleep before they left at first light.

At five thirty he walked on to the stoep the night sky was rapidly retreating as the sun crept towards the horizon. When the others came to the stoep, he instructed them to only drink water, not coffee. This was normal, as on a hunt it could confuse Lindani's sense of smell.

They set off just as the sun rose in the sky and headed on the southeast spoor Lindani had picked up the previous day. Moving on steadily they covered around two kilometres when Lindani called a halt under the shade of an Acacia tree. The rain had washed the entire spoor away, but they had passed under the tree and its branches acted like an umbrella.

"See here, the prints of many shoes," Lindani said, drawing Angus's attention to the ground. He walked to the side of the game trail and parted the scrub, "here two of the same. They follow closely. When I saw these yesterday, they were about one hour behind, but these are now three days old."

Angus studied them; still wonder how he did this. "We might as well return to the station today, we'll go on the north tonight, they're coming from Mozambique that way and go back this way?" Lindani nodded.

When they returned, the sandbag reached a quarter of the length of the front stoep. Soon everyone was filling the flour bags and by mid-afternoon the stoep work was finished, and the hundred- and twenty-centimetre wall enclosed the L shaped stoep.

As the clouds built on the horizon above the hills over the valley, Lindani pointed to the east.

"A storm is coming."

"The dark cumulonimbus clouds were black at the base and boiled like giant white mushrooms at their tops against the blue sky, and the air felt cool as a breeze began to blow down the valley.

The first lightning bolts struck the hills, and the wind had picked up, whipping the tress, as the clouds finally dropped their burden and the rain fell in sheets.

"Good, this storm will wash the ground clean, removing all spoors," Lindani said.

They spent the evening listening to the radio. News from the Rhodesian Broadcasting Corporation came at nine o'clock.

"An attack this afternoon on Silinda missionary. It's known the missionary was staffed by four Belgian couples and three children. Severe storms in the area are hampering any forces reaching the mission," the announcer reported.

Angus switched the radio off and looked at his tracker. "That's twenty kilometres northeast of here."

Lindani nodded. "They're coming, but they will not move in this storm."

They went to the stoep while the storm was still in full swing, the rain pounding on the tin stoep roof, making a curtain of water as it poured from the sloped edge, soaking the flour bags.

CHAPTER 8

*T*hey woke just before day light the air was fresh the smell of vegetation filled the air, the storm passed during the night. The dry season was at end, grass in the compound already showing a thin carpet of green on the red earth.

"Only water this morning" Angus reminded them. They all nodded; they knew they were going hunting today. But it was a different kind of hunt, one none of them had ever been on. The quarry was not animals. Today the quarry was man.

They left the station and skirted the fence heading to the north, then picked up a narrow game trail headed in an easterly direction

Spreading out at the normal ten paces, Lindani led followed by Angus. After four kilometres they reached a wider trail crossing. Lindani signalled to the others to halt. They did so, crouching by the side of the trail, weapons at the ready. The tracker walked slowly around the intersection, head down searching the ground.

He waved the others forward to him. "Elephants, Gazelle

and Leopard, no human prints," he advised, and they moved on, sticking to the narrow trail.

Three kilometres on they reached the banks of the Ugura river, its coffee brown water with cream, white-crested waves raging. It was a spate river that dried out completely from mid-May until August, but now full, its brown water made its annual journey from the mountains to join the Zambezi River two hundred kilometres away.

A game path which was just visible ran parallel along its banks. They headed upriver, where a kilometre further on the river swept in a bend. Lindani suddenly stopped and held his hand up. He stood motionless for a few moments then took two steps back down the trail; he turned and signalled with his hand, his thumb tapping his forefinger, signalling VOICES.

He slipped into the undergrowth to the right of the trail. Angus and the rest of the men hid, easing both left and right. Angus ducked behind a small evergreen blue bush where he could see up the trail as far as the bend. The fore stock on the R1 felt wet in his palm.

A few moments later a figure came in to view on the trail. He was dressed in a camouflage uniform, a rifle slung across his shoulders as if it was a buffalo yoke, with his wrists resting on the weapon. As he walked casually towards him a cigarette hung from his lips, others came in to view in similar fashion. He counted eleven of them.

Angus noticed the leading figure had blue baseball shoes on his feet. Signalling to Chatambuza and Dzingia pointing one way then the other, they sank deeper into the bush. They were going to flush from either side further up the trail.

Lifting his weapon, Angus waited until there was only fifty meters between him and the oncoming group, and taking aim at the leading figure, he focused his shot at the centre of his chest and pulled the trigger. The carbine bucked and the man instantly dropped, thrown backwards by the impact, the round tore into him. He threw the switch to automatic.

Mandala and Manodno joined in the mayhem and when he heard Chatambuza join in with the thundering sound of his ten-bore shotgun, the clash was over in a few seconds. Silence fell again on the trail. Nothing moved in the line of bodies stretched out along the path. Not taking chances, Angus ejected the magazine and loaded a fresh one, before he stepped out from the bush onto the trail again.

As they moved along the line of bodies, they gathered up the weapons they had been carrying; all AK 47s except for one, which none of them had ever seen before, it had a round magazine and tripod.

Suddenly two men appeared on from either side of the trail," they were dressed differently, not in the green camouflage the bodies lying on the ground wore. They had light khaki shorts and shirts, both wore beards, one was a black man, the other was white.

A few meters behind them, Lindani shouted. "Scouts."

"We thought you were fire force," the white man said.

Angus shook his head, but before he could speak the noise of aircraft came from the south, Angus nodded in same direction as the sound of a plane's engines.

"That will be them."

The white scout brought the radio from his back a long khaki coloured military one and spoke into it. "Seeker four abort mission repeat abort mission, do you copy?" the radio crackled back.

"Roger that seeker out."

The scout turned his attention back to Angus again. "Who are you?"

"Game and wildlife from the Nyanga station," Angus replied.

"I heard all that was going on there the other day from the saint's transmissions, these are the bastards who attacked the missionary yesterday they killed everyone even the kids, we have been tracking them that's why we thought you were fire force," the scout replied."

Angus looked puzzled. "Who?"

The scout looked at him "The guys who flew into your station The Saints One Commando Light Infantry they were on fire force."

He nodded in Lindani's direction. "He must be good if he managed to get the drop on Fudzai, he's one of the best trackers in the regiment." Fudzai nodded in agreement. They started to gather up the weapons off the trail and collect the ammunition from the dead.

"What's this?" Angus held up the unusual gun.

"It's a Russian RPD 7.62x39mm the belt is in the drum.

As they piled them in one spot, he posed another question. "Are you going to have these collected?"

The scout replied, "No, we'll destroy them, before we leave. They're no good to us. These all use 7.62x33mm they don't pack as big a punch over a longer range. Ours are all 7.62x51mm NATO rounds same as your R1 they give us longer range. Where are you headed now?"

Angus told him they were returning to the station to replenish their ammunition.

The scout held out his hand. "Dempie Van Rooyen," he said, introducing himself.

"Angus McLean," he responded as they shook hands.

Van Rooyen turned to Fudzai. "Stick some C4 and a fuse in that lot and let's get out of here."

The air was thick with blue blow flies now and the din they were making getting louder, Angus asked, "Can we take that Russian gun and the ammo?"

"You can a have the whole bloody lot." Dempie replied.

Nodding to his men, Angus instructed them to gather up the weapons.

"Where are you heading for now?" Angus enquired.

Dempie told him they were going to head for the Salisbury road see they could pick up a ride back to the barracks to have some R&R and a week off. "Can't wait to have a nice shower and a beer and a decent meal," he added.

"We can supply all of that and a soft bed. The station is only fourteen clicks from here." Both he and Fudzai nodded in agreement. "Chatambuza can take you back to your barracks tomorrow morning, we need to pick some supplies in Salisbury." He turned and looked at the blood-soaked corpses and asked, "What do we do about them?"

Van-Rooyen simply said "leave them where they are they a carrion now."

As he raised his eyes skyward twenty vultures circled effortless against the blue sky. They had gone about a kilometre when they heard the Hyenas yapping and whooping behind them.

CHAPTER 9

They reached the station mid-afternoon, the gates were closed as they had left them when they departed, but now an extra Land Rover was parked next to theirs, the same model, a Safari. They arrived at the gates and moved inside. When they reached the stoep, Louie De-Langa sat at the table, his enormous hands clasped on his chest.

"How are you?" Angus asked.

"Dead... all dead," Louie said, looking up, his red rimmed eyes peering from his dust encrusted face.

Angus dropped a hand to his shoulder. "I know my friend; we share the same grief."

Lindani did the same. "I to share your grief, Louie."

De-Langa sneered at him. "Mr Louie to you kaffir," he snarled.

Lindani removed his hand and walked away, Angus did likewise and they both walked down the hallway and into the kitchen. Lindani sat quietly at the table.

"He's in shock. Let him handle this in his own way, eh? I'll talk to him." Angus told him. The scouts shuffled around the kitchen awkwardly. This was not their problem.

Dzingia had got straight down to lighting the range. The fire was ablaze, and the big coffeepot sat on the iron top. He went to the larder and came back with cold cooked Warthog ham and a cooked joint of Impala. Laying them on the table, he came back again with four bottles of Castle beer then some enamel plates help yourselves.

The two scouts did not need telling twice, Manodno had a big grin spreading on his face they were like kids in a sweet shop they didn't know whether to stuff the cooked meat in their mouths or guzzle the beer.

When everyone had eaten and showered, they sat on the stoep

"Do you have a certain time you have to be back at your barrack's Dempie?," Angus asked Van-Rooyen.

He shook his head. "No, anytime in the next couple of days."

"So, you don't have to be up early?"

"No. Don't forget we have not had a proper night's sleep in three weeks, let alone in a bed," Van-Rooyan reminded him.

After they ate, they sat drinking beer on the stoep they sat in the semi-darkness, another thunderstorm was brewing in the distance, the only light on the stoep came from the office window through the sun filter blinds.

"You guys done really well back there today," Van-Rooyan praised.

Angus shrugged his shoulders and drew a deep breath. "First time I have killed a man."

"Well, don't go beating yourself up they would have done the same to you or some other innocent bugger."

"It's how we hunt animals," Angus shrugged.

De-Langa still sat at the table in silence. Angus got up and went in doors, as he did so the storm broke the rain started pounding against the roof. He came back to the stoop carrying a bottle of brandy and three mugs.

"Sorry we have no glasses all the crockery was smashed in the raid," he said. He poured the brandy into the mugs gave one to Van-Rooyen and put one in front of De-Langa. "Here Louie drink this."

De-Langa picked it up, his hand made the mug look like a thimble and emptied it in one gulp.

"Help yourself," Angus told him, nodding at the bottle. "Fudzai is having a ball in there with the others." Focusing his attention on De-Langa he asked, "Do you want to talk about it? Louie? It might help to get it off your chest."

Louie shook his head and stayed silent.

"Do you originate from South Africa?" he asked, Van-Rooyan.

"My grandfather came here in the nineteen thirties. My father was born here." When I came in here today, I noticed your defences are not up to much," he told him, changing the subject. "If you are going to stay here you are going to beef them up?"

When Angus nodded, Van-Rooyan advised him what measured he'd take to do this.

"Have the vegetation cut back for at least two hundred meters around the fence to get a better field of fire. Get some locals in and get them to cut it back. Get some high vantage points built as a firing position." Pointing to the workshop roof, he jerked his thumb up. "And have the same on this building roof. We will have no trouble tonight in this storm. As the rain pounded down, the darkness intermittently penetrated by flashes of lightning. They come in the dark, usually doing a loop when they come over the border, and back again the following night."

They sat drinking late into the night, before going to bed. Next morning Angus woke just as daylight came. It was still raining, but not as heavy as the previous night. No one else was up and about, so he sat on the stoep alone, having lit the fire in the kitchen and making a pot of coffee.

De-Langa was first to emerge from within. He came and sat the table with a coffee in his hand.

"Sorry about last night," he said, "my head has been up my arse."

"I understand. Take your time and talk when he you're ready, but I think you owe Lindani an apology, Louie."

"What for? "

"Yesterday when he offered his sympathy you bit at him, telling him not to call you Louie but Mr Louie, and you said, 'kaffir'. We don't have any misters or kaffirs on this station, we are all friends.

Louie eyed him and nodded. "I will speak to him later." With that, the others drifted on to the stoep, so the conversation finished there.

The scouts made ready to depart mid-morning; the rain had stopped, and the sun was back. They both shook hands with all the men. Angus told them to radio him first and gave him their frequency to come anytime they were in the area. As they climbed into the Isuzu, Van-Rooyen turned to Angus.

"A present for you," he said, giving him a bag from his back.

"What is it?" Angus asked, looked at the khaki bag.

"Claymore— mine," Van-Rooyan replied as he climbed into the back of the truck. Angus grinned at the whiskey.

They set off Chatambuza with his list of things to get in Salisbury with Manodno sitting beside him. Angus had told them to spend the night in Salisbury and Van-Rooyen assured him they could spend the night at the barracks.

After they'd gone, Angus gathered the rest on the stoep around the table and started giving these instructions, he told Dzingia to with Mandala and go to Nyanga village and see if he could recruit some labour with pangas for cutting the elephant grass and the other foliage back around the compound. He told them when they got the recruits to stay and guard them.

Then he turned to Lindani. "We will start on high firing positions we will raise some roof sheets from the station and workshop."

They all set about their various tasks but Angus and Lindani made no headway. The heat in both roof spaces had felt unbearable so they gave up. Lindani suggested it would be better done at night or early morning before the sun got on the hot tin. Angus agreed and asked Lindani if he could think of anything else, they could do.

"We could cut firing slots in the gable of the buildings; it would give all round protection and might keep the roof spaces and might make it a bit cooler."

"Good idea. Fetch a ladder from the workshop." He did, and they began that task.

In the late afternoon, Dzingia and Mandala returned and said they had help coming the following morning. The clouds had built with the wind growing in strength. They were heading for another storm, but in the early evening, a short sharp shower of rain fell cooling the ground and raising a light mist.

"Come on, let's go into the roof space and check if it's any cooler," he told Lindani. They did, but it wasn't easy as they'd had to stand on the roof spares as the planks of the interior someone had nailed wooden ceiling to them, and their weight would cause them to fall through if they'd stood on those.

As it was dark, Angus had to negotiate his way carefully to a slot they had cut in and peered through a metre long slot, where the boards had been removed.

"Perfect," he said as he made his way from the hatch in the hallway. "We'll have to build some catwalks up there," he told Lindani. "We'll take the kennel apart tomorrow and use that timber. The dogs can sleep on the stoep from now on."

It was a quiet night on the station with only the four of them. Manodno had cooked a guinea fowl, and they ate it with rice, meali-meal, and a chilli sauce because they had no bread, the flour had been ruined in the attack.

"Coffee only tonight. That rain shower was not enough to halt any progress they might be making tonight if they are coming." Angus warned.

The men woke the next morning, and they were eating breakfast around the table when the local help arrived at the gate. Manodno waved and made his way over to them opening the gate. He returned to the stoep to collect his carbine.

As he picked it up, Angus snapped at him. "Don't let that happen again. Do you hear me?"

Manodno looked confused Angus pointed to the R1. "Armed at all times remember?"

Manodno slinked away quietly to the truck as Dzingia came through the front door making a show that he was carrying his. Angus smiled to himself and thought the bugger must have heard me chew Manodno out. He watched them drive out through the gates and Lindani closed them and chained them. Then he and Lindani went to the kennels and let the dogs out for the last time, knowing they would have the run of the compound from now on.

The sky wasn't clear with the broken cloud overhead. The sun only made brief appearances. "Did you order this weather, Lindani?" he asked, as they stripped the wood from the kennels. He grinned when he saw his tracker's frown. "I'm joking, meaning did you speak to god?"

"I speak to the lord every day," Lindani replied without humour.

They worked steadily by mid-day until they had dismantled the kennels and had carried half of the wood up to the station. They stopped for a break.

"We'll finish this roof space first and then the workshop when we're finished," Angus decided.

They turned their attention back to the task in hand, and laid the walkway boards four wide, give the user a path of half a meter wide, and then started on the central platform which was it was a meter wide and two long.

At chest height, where one panel of the sheeting overlapped the other, they eased it and raised up the bottom of the corrugated sheeting along the entire length of the platform at the rear of the roof. When finished they propped them with pieces of the flat kennel wood. Deciding that would do for now, they moved to the front section of the roof and did likewise.

Now the building gave firing points on all points of the compass around it and gave them a view of the locals in the elephant grass hacking away with the pangas.

They moved to the workshop next. The roof space was already floored; they'd already used it to store parts for the vehicles and other maintenance equipment. Using the four pieces of square wood that had been the upright posts of the kennel, they cut them roughly at head height, and loosened the panels. Slipping a piece of the flat wood between the panels and their neighbours, they used the end of two lengths to lift the panels up and prop the piece of flat wood and sheets up.

Angus climbed through the opening on the roof using the hammer and nails he secured the sheets to the flat wood and props, they did likewise on the opposite side now they could cover all sides of the compound, they returned to the main building and repeated the process.

When they'd finished their task, late in the afternoon, they toured the compound. From every point of it they could see more than one of the pill-box-like roof openings. Both men felt it was a job well done.

Chatambuza and Dzingia returned at dusk the Isuzu cage was full, of the basic supplies, bags of flour, coffee, sugar and most importantly thirty cases of Castle and ten rolls of bell wire.

CHAPTER 10

*T*he men still carried out their routine patrols, but only short ones as they did not want to leave the others on the radio alone overnight.

They'd had to shoot the wounded animals Willie Bekker would have treated.

Two days after the foliage had been cleared, they had a two hundred area of clear ground around the compound. They had made eight mines as Ewan had told them to and connected the bell wire to each one so they could be activated individually by touching the bell wires to the car battery terminals.

It had rained most nights as the tropical thunderstorms passed over the Nyanga valley. They had been on short patrols both days but nothing out of the ordinary, all Lindani was could pick up from the ground they covered were animal tracks and places in the grass where animals had been grazing.

He had instructed all his men to place the AK47s and ammunition at the high fire stations and had allocated each position with a radio, and they had always manned the main radio, when a patrol was out.

Dawn was just breaking as he sat on the stoep with a mug of coffee when the two dogs suddenly took off down the stoep stairs to the fence between the workshop and the surgery. He stood up to get a better view at the edge of the clearing in the elephant grass he saw a small red glow then a wisp of smoke rising in the cool morning air. Casually, he walked inside and went straight to the office, picking up his .480.

Edging the sun filter curtain aside with the muzzle and put the scope to his eye. Scanning the area where he had seen the red glow a face filled the scope a white-bearded face. Angus knew the communist countries backed the insurgents trying to get a foothold in Africa. When Angus saw a hand lift a fat cigar to the would-be attacker's mouth, the tip glowed red, and he squeezed the big gun's trigger. Itsf loud bark broke the morning silence, and the face in his scope exploded.

The shot brought the rest of his men running as he ran back to the stoep shouting attack over and over as a swarm of bodies immediately emerged from the edge of the clearing.

Knowing the earth wires from the home-made devices were already attached to the battery he hesitated a few seconds until his quarry advanced towards the mines, and then he touched the positive pole on the battery of the first wire.

With an orange flash the hinged like lid flew off and the debris from the drum cut a scythe like swath toppling the advancing men. Angus touched another wire on the terminal and the grim reaper took another swath of men. The attackers who were left had seen enough and those who could retreated to the cover of the elephant grass.

Bodies lay scattered on the open ground when a single shot fired from the workshop. Angus grabbed the radio mike. "Manodno, Chatambuza who's firing?"

Manodno responded that some of them were still alive and were suffering which reminded Angus how his wife and the rest of them had suffered.

"Let them suffer."

It only took ten minutes for the first vultures to descend from the cloudless early morning sky and strut among the dead and wounded as if spoilt for choice. It wouldn't be long before the other carnivores joined them. Manodno informed him through the radio he'd counted twenty-six bodies on the ground.

A short time later, the feeding frenzy had reached fever pitch. With the number of bodies spread on the open ground, it had allowed all the distinct groups to feed without the usual squabbling. The men stayed at their stations for the rest of the morning, but as the sun rose higher in the sky, the roof spaces became unbearably hot, and when he felt certain the retreating party wouldn't be back, Angus told them to stand down.

Late afternoon, as they sat on the steop, they heard shots in the distance. A lumbering Dakota banked around the side of a hill further down the valley. The firing increased, and then slowly died out except for a few occasional shots.

"Stations," Angus shouted. The alarmed men all took off running to their designated stations where they watched and waited nothing moved in the still after-noon sun.

Their silence was suddenly broken by an explosion in the distance, then silence fell again. Angus began to feel he was slowly being cooked. Sweat oozed from every pour; the sun had turned the roof space in furnace. He wiped his eyes and forehead with his discarded shirt and brought his binoculars back to his eyes— movement! He held his breath as h watched a bush shake, noting there was no wind. It moved again and again, every few seconds. He caught a glimpse of someone in uniform, a khaki uniform. The terrorists they had killed by the river wore green camouflage.

When they came closer, he then saw they had a bag on their backs and were carrying FN rifles not the distinguishing curve of the AK47 magazine: they were Paradaks infantry Paratroopers.

His radio crackled to life. "Nyanga, are you receiving?"

Angus confirmed back he did.

"RLI approaching do not open fire," he confirmed the call and instructed them to come in. Angus told his men not to fire and gather in front of the stoop. As the RLI approached the gates, sixteen of them, one waved his hand in the air, it was Sandy Ewan.

As the men came into the compound, Ewan told them to drop their kit at the front of the house, and head for the shade of the stoop. Manodno brought a big jug of water, a bucket of ice cubes and a tray of enamel mugs.

Eight weeks had passed since Ewan had last been there. He shook hands with Angus and the rest of his men.

"You and you guys are the talk of the town, back at the barracks. Van-Rooyen says you were as good as us in stop kill." He strode over to the corner of the stoop and picked up one of the Argyle combination guns. "What the hell are these?"

Angus told him they were elephant guns, ten bore shotgun and a .460 rifled barrel mounted on top.

One of Ewan's men came over and picked up its partner. "Fur fuck's sake, man. Whit a fuckin tool. Ah widne mind getting in a barney wi wane o these."

"Put it down Morton, you're getting a hard on," Ewan joked. Angus noted as Morton walked away, he was the smallest of the group. "He's a mad bastard. Tried to join the

British army, but they refused him on physiological grounds. The daft fucker bought his own ticket and came here just to join up."

Ewan went on to tell Angus Morton was not his proper name; it was Andy Morgan he came from Greenock and supported Morton football team. "He would never have made a soldier in the British army, but he's a good man to have with you on a contact. Don't know if he's fearless or brainless" Ewan said with a shrug.

Angus asked how long they were going to be at the station.

Ewan shrugged. "When they send transport… it might be today or tomorrow."

Angus told Manodno to take out a haunch of a boar from the fridge and to tell Dzingia to light the fire pit. The stoep was less crowded as some of the men were sitting in the shade on the ground below the stoep.

"Haw Angy gonny giez a shot to wane o them cannons?" a voice shouted.

Ewan smiled and shook his head. "Wondered how long he would take. He won't give you peace now." He picked up one of the Argyles. "Come on then," Angus replied.

A few of the other men followed him as he led them through the gates and over the edge of the open ground where the vegetation started at around forty metres. He stopped and pointed to a big cactus plant.

Angus held the Argyle on its side, pointing to the single trigger in its trigger guard. "That's the rifle trigger." He then pointed to the two triggers behind it. "These are the shotgun triggers. The toward one fires first, then the left barrel. It has a full choke, that keeps the shot concentrated. Just hit the triggers from front to back." Morton nodded. "And keep it tight it's got a heavy recoil," he warned him. "First shot on the left leaf, second main body where it joins, third main trunk close to the ground, and take those sunglasses of if you want to keep wearing your face." Morton nodded and pushed his sunglasses to the top of his head.

The first shot tore a hole in the meaty leaf blowing the back of it out, and his sunglasses lenses shattered as they hit the ground. The second created a hole in the trunk the size of a dinner plate. The final shot struck just above ground level and cut the trunk clean like a knife. The cactus toppled over. Morton stood staring ahead of him as if in a trance. Angus reached and took the gun from him.

"Whit a fuckin tool," he said in awe. "Where kin ah buy wan o these?"

Angus told him they were made specially for one of his predecessors.

"Calm down Morton or you'll come in your drawers." One of the other men who had come to watch shouted.

"He'd end up trying to shag the thing if he had one," another of Ewan's men joked.

"How the fuck did it that cut the trunk clean?" Morton asked.

Angus he told him the rifle bullets weighed eight ounces and travel at thirteen hundred feet per second and because of their soft nose they spread on impact.

"The first shotgun cartridge is a number one eight lead balls, weighing nine ounces, but we open them, and drip melted tallow in the casing, that holds the shot together, so they don't spread. The third is the same cartridge, we take half of the shot out, cut a slot on in with a knife and crimp them on a half meter length of chrome fuse wire, one pellet his and the others wrap around turning it to a cheese wire." Morton was in awe.

"You didn't listen to me," Angus said, nodding at his shattered sunglasses, but Morton was still mesmerised.

When Angus told Ewan about Morton's sunglasses, Ewan

shrugged. "That's what I mean when I said he would never make a soldier. He failed to get into the British army, when they asked him at his interview why he wanted to become a soldier when they asked him why he told them he wanted to kill people." Angus raised a brow and Ewan sighed. "So... he saved up the airfare to come here. He was a bit of an eejit, but not as bad as some of the guys who were in the regiment."

Ewan's men came from all over Australia, Canada, most European countries. He told Angus they made up around forty percent of the regiment. Some Yanks and Aussies had fought against the Vietcong and had passed on their tricks to the rest of the regiment.

"What do you mean by tricks?" Ewan explained booby traps like taking the nitro out of an AK shell and replacing it with plastic explosive, putting it back in mag and throwing it back where they found. It has a great result because our 7.62 round is 51mm long they use 33mm long and 39mm for the RPD. The insurgents try to use it when they come across it and it's usually second or third round in the mag. The enemy gets a face full of gun bits, so tell your men not to use any ammo they find lying around. The insurgents do the same with mortar shells that usually take out the whole crew, and RPG rounds that remove the head and most of their upper body and anyone else around.

CHAPTER 11

The scent in the air was of roast hog, Manodno came out with 6 fresh baked loaves. They only had a few plates, but the soldiers compromised they took the lining out of their jump helmets and used the metal outer as a bowl. They sat on the ground, eating around the fire pit.

"What happened to the other white guy you had here?" Ewan asked.

He nodded towards the house. "De-Langa? He's in his room. He's still taking it badly, doesn't say much and won't part take in anything. He sits in his room most of the time."

"How are you coping?" Ewan asked.

"Still hurting but keeping busy. At least I saw my wife's body… bad as it was. But De-Langa didn't see his as her body was cremated. They set the house station on fire after they had killed them." Ewan nodded, remembering he had been one of the soldiers who had responded.

"It doesn't seem right sitting around the fire pit without a beer. Want one?" The light was just fading. "Okay," Ewan said, laughing, "but just the one. We'll be owing you an entire pub if we keep this up." He nodded at his men. "They won't be going anywhere tonight, anyway"."

Angus told him they had plenty. "You can have two each," he said.

"Two and no more," Ewan replied. Angus instructed Monodno to fetch the beers and a cheer went up from Ewan's men.

"Two each and I'm paying for it. You lot can all pay me when you get back to barracks."

Ewan reached into his shirt pocket and took out three ten-dollar bills and handed them to Angus. When he tried refusing them, Ewan told him thirty-two beers would cost more in a Salisbury bar. When they had finished drinking, Angus told Ewan's men some could sleep on the first floor of the workshop with the rest on the stoep.

Later that night when he and Ewan sat on the stoep, Angus asked if he could do him a favour. Ewan nodded.

"When you get back to your barracks, could you give the department of game a call for me? I'm worried about De-Langa. I think he needs psychiatric help. I don't want to call it in myself, because Louie would just go ape shit. But if it comes from the department, he'll go. He's an Afrikaner he won't challenge authority." Ewan nodded in agreement.

The night passed quietly and next morning they were all up and about, all except Louie. Ewan's radio came to life informing group five, they would be picked up, and that two choppers were on the way. Another voice answered the call with a short answer of "Copy." Ewan nodded towards the workshop "that's us."

The whole of group five had ended up sleeping in the workshop, and those still there crossed over to the main building. Manodno had poured coffee into the mugs and had bread and honey on the table when they reached the stoep.

One of them asked if Ewan if he'd copied the radio message. Ewan nodded.

"Angus, this is Olaf Bass, he's five stop's, troop leader."

Angus shook the man's hand. "Better get your guys on the stoep, there's some food there and coffee."

Bass answered him in heavily accented English. "Thank you, it might be the first and last today."

The men didn't waste any time finishing off the bread and coffee. Manodno came back with eight packages of left-overs from the previous night's dinner, wrapped in greaseproof, paper some.

"Thanks," Bass said sounding grateful.

Ewan countered "Eh, have you lot not got a wee pressie for these guys?

"Oh yes," A German man replied. He told Morton to get the things they'd brought for the contact yesterday.

Morton and returned with a green backpack and placed it on the table. "Swap ye this lot fir wane o they cannons." He joked, smiling at Angus. Morton emptied the bag's contents on the table.

"Forty AK magazines." Angus asked, shook his head, and smiled.

"Ach bit wait, thures mer," Morton said as he retreated from the stoop again.

"I thought your accent was broad, Morton's is far worse. How do the rest of your team understand him?"

"They don't but he talks shite most of the time anyway," Ewan replied with a grin.

Morton returned to the stoop with another RPD and two magazines. "wit aboot it noo?" Morton asked Angus in regards to the Cannon. Angus still shook his head. Morton raised an eyebrow. "Ach you bluudy teuchters are aw the same." He smiled.

The two helicopters arrived and came into land.

As soon as they touched down, Bass shouted above the engine noise. "Okay mount up."

The first lot of troops had their packs on their backs and doubled over as they ran to avoid the blades. Seconds later they were gone.

As they waited for Ewan's team's transport, Angus asked him if he knew where they were going. He told him they never knew until they were airborne only the pilot knew, and it was never sent out over the air. "The little man what country is he from, he speaks a language I do not know?" Lindani asked Angus.

Angus burst out laughing. "He's Scottish."

"But he speaks differently from you. Is he from another tribe?"

Angus chuckled. "Something like that," he replied.

Ewan's radio came to life again thirty minutes later. "Stop group three, stand by for pick up in twenty minutes."

"That's us," Ewan said. "Awright lads get yer shite the gather."

As the two helicopters approached, Angus and Ewan shook hands with all the men. He reminded him about the call to the game office and he confirmed his agreement to do that. With same procedure as before, they bordered the helicopters as soon as they touched down and were gone.

The next six weeks passed uneventfully, Louie De-Langa still stayed in his room, he would only wash when told to, and came and took his food to the room. Manodno was complaining he had to keep going into his room and bringing his plate, mug, and leftover food back to the kitchen.

They carried out their routine patrols, but only short ones as they did not want to leave the others on the radio alone overnight. They had been shooting animals Willie Bekker would have treated.

CHAPTER 12

*T*hey returned from a patrol one day and a big crocodile sat in front of the house, not of the reptilian species, this one had originated in South Africa, it was an armoured transporter with its V-shaped bottom, designed to deflect the blast from the countless land mines the insurgents planted on dirt roads.

It rode high off the ground, with its fifty-calibre machine gun mounted on a circular rail to give the operator a three hundred and sixty degree field of fire.

They parked the Land Rover alongside the bigger vehicle. Skirting around the front, and up the steps on to the stoep, there were five people sitting around the table. Through the open front door, Angus noticed four other men in the kitchen at the end of the hall.

He headed for the table on the stoep, the others from the patrol group headed for the kitchen. At the table they were all seated except one Louie De-Langa was leaning against the side of the building, arms folded across his chest. As he approached it the table two of the men got up and left.

Ted Hibbins head of a department in the Salisbury office

stood and shook Angus's hand as he did so he introduced Doctor Harris he is head medical adviser. Angus shook his hand. The remaining stranger stayed seated, their back to where Angus stood.

"This is Doctor Vandekamp, the replacement vet." As Vandekamp stood up and removed the bush hat, a long blonde ponytail dropped to the waist. She turned to face him, her head just above the level of his chin as he had his hand ready to shake hers.

He hadn't expected a female. The young woman looked up into his eyes and he froze, mesmerised by her stare. Her emerald eyes were like pools of lime jelly. She was beautiful, her tanned skin and white teeth of her smile matched perfectly with her blonde hair, highlighting the colour and depth of her eyes. She took his hand and shook it, but his eyes were locked on her gaze.

"Doctor Harris has come to give you and Louie the once over… just to make sure the horrendous experience you've had is not affecting you." Angus nodded, still holding her hand.

"Is there anywhere he could examine you in private?" the doctor asked.

Angus suggested the office and Harris asked if he minded being first. When Angus agreed, Harris picked up his bag from the floor beside the table and followed him. Once inside the office, the doctor asked about De-Lange's behaviour.

"He won't wash unless we make him. He sits in his room all the time, even to eat. He comes and collects his food, takes it in there, letting plates of food rot. His temper is very short with the Shonas." Doctor Harris wrote it all down.

"How are you bearing up?"

"I'm hurting like hell but managing for the others. I'm kept busy."

When the two men had finished, Doctor Harris asked him to send De-Langa in.

Angus went to the stoep and sent him over. When he had gone in with Harris, Ted turned to Angus.

"We're taking him with us tonight." Angus felt relieved De-Langa would have some help.

Ted, he told them they'd had a construction team at Matazari, they had been there three weeks and had most of the work finished. He told him the two guys who had left the table when he had arrived were Fran Murphy and Tom McCabe. They were going to run Matazari, and Annika Vandekamp would work between the two stations, as had Willie Bekker.

A short time later Harris led Louie onto the stoep, announcing he had agreed to go to Fort Victoria for a few tests. Within an hour, the Crocodile was only visible as a dust cloud as it climbed the rise towards Nyanga.

They had stood on the stoep watching it as it diminished into the distance; he turned to Manodno and asked him to take Doctor Vandekamp's bag to his room; she raised her eyebrows and cocked her head to one side.

"So, we share a room?" Angus stuttered.

"N... N... No. You can have my room until we get the room De-Langa was in cleaned and the bedding washed."

She flashed him a look he couldn't decipher and nodded.

"Annika please call me Annika you had me wondering there." He felt his face flush. Why did he feel like a stuttering schoolboy around her?

"I'll show you around tomorrow morning as the sun was about to slip below the hills to the west."

When they ate that night, a very unusual event took place. All his men ate at the table he didn't have to think to hard what the reason for that was.

After dinner, Angus sat on the stoep alone with Annika;

the rest of his men had satisfied their curiosity. It felt strange to have female company again, and Angus was stuck for words.

Attempting conversation. he asked. "Did Ted Hibbins not tell you it was dangerous here in the bush?" She nodded. "Then why put yourself at risk?" Annika shrugged but didn't reply. "There're no animals on the station now, only the two dogs and domestic animals," he told her. "You're South African right?"

She shook her head and smiled, her eyes glittering in amusement. "No, I'm from the Netherlands, from Utrecht." Annika went on to tell him she had qualified at the university of Rotterdam.

"What made you to come to Rhodesia?"

"I came with my husband."

Angus had noticed the ring on the third finger of her right hand as they ate.

"Divorced?" he asked as he nodded towards the ring.

Her smile was a sad one. "No. My husband was killed eight months ago." Annika paused as her eyes filled with unshed tears. "He drove over a land mine." She got up and walked over to the stoep rail and leaned on it. Staring out into the darkness. "Ted told me what happened here. I'm sorry for you."

"If you know about that, why have put yourself at risk by coming out here into the bush?"

He could sense by the change in her voice she was crying. Annika stood facing away from him for a while, and Angus didn't know what to do. Did he comfort her? He had only met the woman, so he decided he'd wait until she sorted herself out, and he sat in silence. Eventually she sniffed and turned wiping her eyes with the back of her hands.

"I am sorry" she said he told her, there was no need to apologise inside he knew he had wanted to join in with her tears. "I came here knowing it was dangerous, but after my husband was killed, I just don't care anymore."

He vanished inside and came back with a bottle of brandy and two mugs. He poured some out and handed it to her. "Drink this," he told her. She took a mouthful and swallowed. A shudder ran through her body.

"Brandy. I only ever drink wine… now I remember why," she smiled.

Angus told her they only had that or Castle lager on the station. Then told her he'd ask Manodno to bring wine with the next supplies. He poured and swallowed a measure, then poured himself another.

"Can you make mine a Castle?" Annika asked. Angus nodded, went back inside, and came back with one in a clean mug. "No glass?" she asked, taking the mug from him.

"They were all smashed when we got raided."

She frowned and took a swig. "Cheers," she said, shrugging off his comment. "Ted told me you and the others have had to kill men out here." He nodded "I haven't used a gun before, can you show me how?"

He nodded, knowing she may have had to for her own protection or to put a wounded animal out of its misery. "When you have settled in." Angus drunk two more brandies.

"Do you breed?" she asked. His brain went to the gutter, and he stared blankly towards her.

"What?" She smiled and asked again. "Breed? Do you breed man?" Still, he stared. His brain had stopped working. "Do you have a conservation program?" he blinked and shook his head, catching up with her train of thought.

"No, we're a holding station. The breeding program runs at Matazari." He noted she'd her beer.

"Right, we should get to bed." Annika cocked her head to the side and flashed him a toothy white smile. She raised her eyebrows.   "We?"

"I mean not... not me and you, I mean... I mean you must be tired." Fuck shut up Angus.

She gave him a good natured smiled. "Goodnight, Angus."

After saying goodnight, he went to Lindani's room, laid on the sofa, and thanks to the brandy, a few minutes later he passed out.

CHAPTER 13

*N*ext morning, he woke and went to the stoep Manodno had a pot of coffee on the table; he asked who wanted scrambled eggs they all nodded; he poured a coffee and as he drank

"I thought I had a samba sleeping on my sofa last night." Lindani said, and they all laughed.

It stopped when Annika came out on to the stoep. She was dressed in a pair of shorts and an olive-green vest, the Africans all looked away in embarrassment. They weren't used to seeing a white woman exposing so much of her body, as the older colonials had been very reserved.

Angus tried not to stare at her hourglass figure and her long shapely legs, then noticed her braless round breasts beneath the tight cotton vest, and shorts that were just that short! They had barely enough material to reach her thighs. Gone were the sober field jacket, long trousers and boots she had been wearing on her arrival at the station.

"Good morning" she said, breezily.

"Good morning," they all replied.

To distract himself, Angus began barking orders, telling

them Lindani would be leading the patrol that day Manodno and Dzingia would clean out the room De-Langa had been using. He himself would remain in camp and install the new radio in the roof space above the workshop.

After they ate breakfast, they set about their various tasks. He took Annika over to the vet's surgery, showing her where she would be working. She did a quick inventory at the medicine cabinet she made a list of drugs she would need as well.

They left the surgery and walked towards the holding pens.

"Does the way I dress offend you or your men?" Angus struggled for an answer.

"Well, it was a bit of a surprise. I mean, after how looked when you arrived yesterday, dressed in trousers and bush shirt." Annika didn't reply, and the pause made Angus fill the void. "But it was a pleasant surprise." She smiled. "I mean, we've not had a female company around the station for three months now."

Annika appeared to accept his answer and asked what the other buildings were. He pointed out the workshop building, explaining it was used as the skinning station and butcher's room.

Next, he took her to the roof space in the workshop and showed her the defensive positions they had made. She looked out from all four firing positions, pausing at the opening that looked away from the gate.

Angus went over to where she was, but kept his distance, and pointed out they had cleared all the vegetation back further from the fence. We've done the same in the main building. I can show you later if you like." She nodded. "If anything happens here, this where you make for Okay?"

Annika agreed as they walked out of the workshop. Into the sunlight. Her skin was glistening with sweat, and her vest was stuck to her body like a second skin. He could see her nipples protruding under the cotton, and cursed himself, thinking he should have waited until they'd had a cloudy day.

As they headed towards the skinning station, he dared not look in her direction. When they went inside the building the blue electric fly killer lit the room, Angus put on the light and pointed to the two white doors.

"That's the hanging refrigerator and that one's the freezer." He stood by the door as she opened the walk-in refrigerator door and had a look inside. The condensation spilled out as when the cold air met the heat. She slammed the big door shut and came back to where he stood by the door.

Shit! He'd done it again. Annika's nipples were now standing proudly with the cold air. She noticed him looking at them and glanced down.

"Oops," she said, pulling the vest away from her skin.

Angus felt embarrassed and his face reddened.

"I have to get that radio installed in the workshop," he muttered, turned away quickly and said and headed for the main building.

He spent an hour in the sweltering heat of the workshop. He's planned to do that later in the day when it had cooled down, but the heat was less painful and more comfortable than he had felt with Annika. At least she could not torment him there.

When he was finished, he sat in the shaded side of the workshop to cool down, staying there an extra half an hour, staring out at the bush. Eventually, he got up and sauntered to the main building she was not on the stoep good. Going to the fridge in the kitchen, he poured a mug of iced tea and returned to the stoep.

"The lady vet will not let us clean the room," Manodno informed him.

"Why not?" he asked.

"We did it, but she said it wasn't right."

"What isn't right?" he asked, stood, and went inside. The door to De-Langa's old room was closed. Angus knocked and heard her shout to come in. He opened the door and found Annika on her knees, with a brush in her hand, scrubbing the hardwood floor.

"This place needs a woman's touch."

He noted her hair was stuck to her face where strands had escaped from the ponytail. The vest she'd worn was gone, but she had changed into a bright orange body tube with a piece of cloth, sewn onto two elasticated bands to hold it in place over her breasts. She was still wearing the shorts on, her flat tanned midriff glistening with sweat. "If I'm honest, the whole place needs cleaning properly" she stated.

Angus backed out of the door, only too happy to put space between them, and headed back along the corridor. He stopped at his own room and opened the door; she was right. The red dust had replaced the glossy finish on the furniture and clung to the sun filter and mosquito nets. Closing the door again, he called for Manodno.

He told Manodno to go to Nyanga the following day, and see if he could hire a few women, or better still see if he could get two couples, man, and wife. He instructed them to offer them fifty dollars a month and their food and keep. Angus thought the wives could be housekeepers and their men could do the general work about the compound.

He had no idea why he hadn't thought of it before. Hired help would free up Manodno and Dzingia and let them go back to what they were supposed to be there for. Better still, he could send out two patrols each day.

Angus was still sitting on the stoep when Annika came and sat facing him. She had showered and changed into a bright orange shirt. Her long hair was still wet and tied neatly back in a ponytail. The scent of her filled the air, not an overpowering perfume, but a faint fruity smell.

"Sorry I didn't let the men clean my room."

"No, you're right. I guess I wasn't paying much attention since…" he trailed off, not wanting to think about Morag and what had gone on. "I'm sending Manodno and Dzingia to find us help.

"I'm also sorry about the other thing as well," she said and must have seen his puzzled look when she added, "what had happened in the workshop and skinning station."

Knowing instantly what she had referred to Angus's face flushed, and he wondered if she was deliberately trying to embarrass him. He stared at the table like a schoolboy, not knowing how to reply.

Annika got up and leaned across the table and ruffled his hair. "Friends?" she said she went on to explain. "In the Netherlands we are taught not to be ashamed of their bodies, men there would have taken no notice of her like that."

"I didn't mean to stare at you," he replied, nodding at her breasts. She smiled, and he realised he'd gestured at them with his head and wanted the stoep to open and swallow him up.

"If it pleases you, I don't mind," she replied laughing and shook her head.

Angus felt relieved to hear the engines of the two vehicles approaching, he needed a diversion. He rose to his feet and went down the stairs. The Land Rover approached the house, but the Isuzu went straight towards the holding pens.

"What have you got?" he asked, Lindani. "A young wilder beast. We found it crouched in the long grass. It's only about a day old, lions killed its mother."

Annika headed straight for the holding pen. One of the others got it out of the back of the truck. She went into the pen and began inspecting the terrified animal. Manodno had fetched a bowl filled with water and placed it on the ground in front of the small animal. It drank greedily, then went and lay down in the shelter out of the sun. The vet then went to her surgery and came back with a feeding bottle full of dried milk mixed with water and fed the young calf.

When the calf was settled and dinner made, they all ate at the stoep table. Since the female vet had arrived, the rest of the men had retreated to the kitchen table as soon as dinner was over, leaving him alone with Annika.

"When will you reach me to shoot?" she asked as they each sipped a Castle beer.

He thought for a moment. "Tomorrow?"

Annika noted his awkwardness around her. "Why do you feel embarrassed, Angus?"

As he fought to keep his foot out of his mouth, he went on to tell her about the strict upbringing he'd had in the north of Scotland.

"Nudity is frowned upon where I was brought up. The church made the strick rules we lived by and no one dared break them. Even the shop in the village closed on a Sunday, no one worked or played on a Sunday. The sabbath was reserved for church in the morning and again in the evening, with bible readings at the table in between.

She told him in the Netherlands church was also impor-tant but not that strict, but they were very liberated. She went on to tell him Yannie, her husband, was not her first boyfriend; she had two before she met him, but she'd married him six years before, when she was twenty.

Angus was glad of the low light on the stoep and felt his face flush again when did the maths— she was twenty-six, three years older than him. Feeling brave, he spoke about his late wife, telling Annika how he had known Morag all his life. She had gone to the school in the village with him and had been a year older.

They were on their second beer when she stunned him into silence by asking, "Do you miss the comfort of a woman?" Shaking off his embarrassment he answered, honestly.

"Morag was the only woman I ever slept with." After he'd answered, he second guessed himself and thought he'd mistaken what she'd meant by her question.

"Only one girl? I'd two boyfriends before I met Yannie."

"And you slept with them?" Fuck, why did I ask that?

She flashed a cheeky smile and nodded. "I slept with the first one when I was seventeen his name was Per Muller."

He sat in silence, not knowing how to respond for a moment before he reminded her about the prudish ways of his church.

"Where I come from, girls have to save themselves until they get married.

"So, your wife was still a virgin on your wedding night? And you? She asked, her eyebrows raised and tilted her head. The conversation felt intrusive, and he lowered his gaze to the ground without responding.

"Did you wife have a nice body?"

Erm, "I'd never seen her naked in the daylight. We dressed for bed in different rooms, it was the way both of our parents had done."

"You're joking, right?" she asked, but when she saw how mortified Angus looked, she realized he spoke the truth. "How long were you married?" she asked.

"Four years," he replied. A pang of hurt tugged his heart that Morag was gone.

"And you never saw her naked?" she blurted.

He shook his head, and Annika gave him a look of disbelief.

"What about here? What did you wear in bed?"

Angus found her question intrusive but shrugged. "Shorts and a T-shirt.

Uncomfortable with how the conversation was going, he got up from the table, told her he was tired and was heading to bed, and said goodnight to her.

When he reached his bedroom door, he closed it and leaned back against it, eyes pointed to the ceiling eyes and screwed tight shut. The silence in the room felt like a sanctuary from Annika's scrutiny of him.

He went to bed but did not sleep until the early hours of the morning. Instead, he lay and thought back on their conversation. Annika was like a cat playing with a mouse. He thought of the answers he should have given her, which drove him crazy until he eventually fell asleep.

After Lindani took the patrol out the next morning, Angus was in the office updating his records when Annika knocked on the open door.

"Are you busy?" she asked.

He told her he would be free in another ten minutes, and once he'd finished what he was doing, he went to the stoep.

"What can I do for you?" he asked when he found her seated at the table.

"Well... we can begin with you teaching me how to shoot for a start," she said, flashing him her perfect smile.

Angus felt the hot flush rising in his neck.

"Not dressed like that, he thought," he said, trying to be bold.

"What do you mean? What do I have to be dressed like to shoot?"

"Well, for start you can't go out in that outfit." Annika glanced at the yellow body tube with the big frill around the neckline, and a pair of strappy sandals.

"Why?"

"The cartridge cases are hot when they're ejected. You

could get burned if one lands on your feet or down there," he remarked, pointing to her breasts.

She smiled and looked down at her breasts, then raised her eyebrows. "We wouldn't want that, would we?" Angus felt he'd won the argument when she smiled. "Okay, if I change will you show me how to do it?"

She left and chanced, then came back with the outfit she'd worn when he had first met her, bush shirt, long shorts and bush boots.

"Better?" She asked, holding her hands out by her sides for Angus to check her outfit.

He nodded "Much. Okay, let's go."

They left the station by the main gates and walked around to the back of the compound. He stopped and pointed down to the length of the perimeter wire.

"Never shoot if you can't see behind the target unless you have to."

Drawing his Glock nine-millimetre pistol from his back holster, he held it out for Annika to look at.

"This is the butt," he told her, pointing towards it. Next, he showed her how to eject the magazine. "To load it, you slip this into this slot and make sure you ram it home. Next pull back the cocking slide, press the safety to off and fire. It will eject here, and you don't need to cock it again, just fire, it'll keep rejecting until the clip is empty.

"Okay, I think I have got it."

Angus he handed her the pistol, and she ejected the magazine. "I hold its butt, slip this in the slot and make sure it is rammed home." She grinned suggestively, "pull its cock, take the safety away and fire. When I fire, it will eject every time until it is spent."

Every part of the sequence had sounded sexual to Angus, and he felt embarrassed again.

Annika glanced from the gun to him and smiled. "Is that the way to do it?"

His face was crimson, his heart racing, and he took a calming breath. "Yes. Now take a few shots so that we can get back to the shade," he told her, trying to pass off his red face due to the heat.

"Can you show me how you would like me to hold it?" Annika's voice sounded flirty.

Will she ever give up on her suggestive questions? "Just hold it out at arm's length with both hands and fire.

Annika did as Angus suggested, but when the cocking slide went back, it caught the web of skin at the base of her thumb and jammed. When she let out a cry of pain, he ran over to her and eased the slid back, freeing the trapped skin. That'll teach you to be cocky. He thought.

"That's the first time I have been bitten by a cock," she joked with a grin.

Angus tried to ignore her comment. "Shall we do it again?"

After she rubbed her hand and ensured it was okay, he stepped back, and she tried again.

When she'd fired off the rest of the clip, Angus waved her over.

"I think that's enough for one day," he told her.

"Can I try a bigger one next time we do it?" He was sure she knew the effect she'd had on him when she grinned and dropped her gaze to the ground as they walked back towards the gate.

Angus decided he had to fight fire with fire. "You're not ready to try anything bigger."

Annika, she stopped and turned on him and began walking ahead of him backwards.

"How do you know I'm not ready for something bigger unless you try me?"

Tormented by sexual innuendo Angus, shook his head but stayed silent. Was this woman sent here to try me? Is this another of God's tests?

Deciding the best way to deal with Annika was to avoid her. So that night after dinner he went and sat at the kitchen table with the others. Undeterred she joined all of them.

"What are we going to do tomorrow, Angus?" Not spend another day like today, he thought.

CHAPTER 14

*A*ngus suggested Annika went on patrol with Lindani and the others. Manodno and Dzingia were to go Nyanga and see if they could buy some maize and sugar, while they tried to get help. When the men began drifting away from the table, Angus excused himself, saying he wanted an early night, and went to his rooms with a beer.

The following morning with everyone gone was glad to be alone on the station until the early afternoon when the Land Rover came back. Four people sat in the rear seats. When they'd all got out in front of the house, Manodno introduced them.

"This is Banele and his wife, Busani." Angus shook their hands. "And this is Dakaria and his wife, Dova." Again, he shook their hands.

"I'm Angus." After introductions, he told Manodno to take them to the kitchen, give them some food and drink, and show them where everything was. Manodno came back to the stoep with two mugs of iced tea.

"They are good workers, Angoos. My family said so."

"After they've eaten, get Dzingia to take the two men to

the workshop. Give them tools and they can use the corrugated tin from the kennel roof. They can build two rooms on the ground floor of the workshop for themselves. Then get the two women to start cleaning the kitchen proper.

The men got busy, and Angus hadn't heard the others arrive back from patrol; the noises coming from the workshop had drowned out their engines. His eyes gravitated to the rear of the Land Rover, where Annika sat as they drove straight to the surgery. Once they had his attention, he'd stood on the stoep and watched as the men lifted a cheetah from the rear of the Isuzu and carried it into the building. It occurred to him to go over, but Angus decided to keep his distance from his vet.

Later, he was still alone on the stoep when she came over from the surgery. Before she'd sat down, Angus called out for Busani.

She came to his aid immediately. It was a promising start.

"Could you bring some iced tea please and ask Dova and your husbands to come here?"

"These are our new helpers," Angus said when they came to the stoep. "This is Annika. She is the vet here."

Both women bent a little at the knee. "Pleased to meet you, Missy."

"No Missy here, Annika is fine."

They bent at the knee again. "Yes, Bwana."

He frowned and fingered his chest. "Angus," he said, then pointed at the vet. "Annika." they all smiled.

"Yes, Bwana." Angus shook his head as they all turned and left the stoep.

At dinner that evening, Annika told him she'd had removed a cyst from the cheetah's stomach and would keep it in the surgery for a few days until the wound healed, before turning it loose again.

Dova interrupted the conversation when she came to the

table with a Picher of iced tea. When she leaned over to place it on the table, her loose-fitting top, her breasts hung a few inches away from his face. Angus tried not to notice and poured a mug of tea.

After dinner he found himself on his own with Annika, trying not to say too much. "Something puzzles me," she blurted.

"What's that?"

"The sight of my breasts embarrassed you, even though they were under my vest, but you never blinked an eye when Dova nearly stuck hers in your face."

Angus almost choked on his beer. "That's different. It's their way here in the bush."

"Their way? It was a woman's breasts, and they were naked."

Angus felt she was going to him, and he was trapped. "Wear the bloody vest I don't care."

"Oh, don't worry, I will. And you can stare at them all you want. I don't care either." A silent pause fell between them, and Angus's heart raced as stared at each other before they both started laughing.

Once the ice was broken like that, they'd both sat chatting about nothing in particular. He had thought of offering her a beer, but then thought drinking was a dangerous move, they'd found a comfortable level of conversation and he hadn't wanted to give her the chance to start on him again.

* * *

THE RAINS CAME as the bubbling clouds gathered heavier each day until they and weeks rolled into months. Animals came and went on the station, and they'd had no problems with insurgents.

One day when Annika was busy in her surgery using

Dova as her assistant and the two patrols were out for the day, Angus was sitting in the office when the radio crackled to life.

"McLean, are you there? Come in." The Glaswegian voice asked.

Angus lifted his radio and held it near his face. "Receiving."

"Two scouts coming in E.T.A one hour."

"Copy that," Angus replied and placed his radio back on his desk. At first, he wondered if it was Ewan, but he that didn't make sense, Ewan wasn't a scout. After the contact, Angus headed down to the surgery and told Annika they were having company, telling her it was scouts.

Angus was sitting on the stoep when they arrived, two white men: a tall one and a short one. Then a voice rang out at the gate. "Haw Angy, it's me," but it wasn't the voice on the radio. He watched Dakaria open the gate and let them in.

"Gled tey see yi again, Angy, Morton said when they came to the stoep. As they shook hands, he pointed to his partner. "This is Jimmy McGovern." Jimmy offered his hand and Angus shook it.

The contrast between the two men was stark. With Morton being slim and only about five foot six, his partner was the same height as Angus at six feet. He was older. Angus guessed about thirty-five, with mousy brown hair starting to show grey on his sideburns and beard. He was lean, but not thin, and his handshake was firm.

They were sitting in the shade of the stoep. When Annika came out of the surgery, Morton rose to his feet.

"Who the fuck is that? She's a stunner."

"The station vet," Angus replied, feeling instantly protective.

"Windne mind slippin her a length."

"Mind yer mouth an' yer manners," McGovern snapped.

Annika came into the stoep and Angus introduced them to her. They shook their hands.

"When did you move over to the scouts?" Angus asked Morton, distracting him from eye fucking the vet.

"Ach that big German cunt wis nivver aff ma back, kept ordirin me aboot; Morton dae this, Morton dae that... Morton, always fuckin Morton." McGovern reminded him about his mouth, but he took no notice. "Well anyhow, one day we wis hivin a barney an' he says to me if I don't like it, why don't I go for selection as the scouts, they seem tae dey wit they like when they want, so ah did." Morton finished his explanation with a wave of his arms and little bow like a stage artiste.

"Hopeless," McGovern said, rolled his eyes, and then asked Angus if he had any way of letting the regiment know they were there. Angus told him he could call the four-man police station in Nyanga, informing him they had a telephone there.

McGovern asked him when he did, not to mention they were scouts. Angus got up and went to the radio in the office, tuned the dial and asked if he was being received. A UK Brummie accent came back. It was Jack Jones. Angus asked him to call Sally and tell her a package was here for her. They sat on the stoep and talked all evening. Annika whispered to Angus at one point she couldn't understand Morton. I smiled because she'd sat nodding while Morton rattled on about his adventures. McGovern just sat shaking his head, tolerating his colleague.

Annika stood. "I'm going to check on the lioness that was brought in that afternoon."

"Wit happened?" Morton asked.

"She'd be mauled by a big male as she tried to protect her cubs.

"Are you takin her oot, Angy?" I chuckled.

McGovern shook his head. "Listen to you, ya fuckin clown. Whit dea ye mean takin her oot? Where the fuck is he gonny take her? In case ye huvent noticed we're in the fuckin middle of fucking naewhere."

Morton nodded, "Oh aye ah see whit ye mean," he replied, laughing.

"Aw right, yer shagging her int ye, Angy?" he asked just as Annika came on the stoep behind him.

Angus slammed his right into Morton's left temple/ Morton fell off the bench and lay still on the floor. Angus jumped up, half expecting McGovern to defend his partner, but he chuckled.

"That wis a fuckin cracker you jist beat me tae it."

"Are you not going to help him?" Annika asked. She looked down at Morton, still unconscious.

McGovern shrugged his shoulders. "He got doon there by himself he kin get up by himself."

"You two can bed down here on the stoep," Angus said as he stood to go to bed.

"McGovern glanced at Morton. "He looks comfortable where he is, I'll kip on that bench."

* * *

ANGUS WAS first to wake and started the cooking range fire, filling the coffeepot and waited for it to boil. It was still dark as he sat drinking his coffee at the kitchen table, basking in the silence.

Suddenly a thought came into his head. He got up and walked into the office, checking the calendar, noting Christmas was in two weeks. His thoughts turned to Morag. She always loved Christmas. He let out a long sigh.

Stepping out the kitchen door, he went and stood by her grave.

"Almost Christmas, Morag," he said into the darkness. "I miss you dearly, but I'm happy for you at the same time. At least you don't have to go through this bloody war. Forgive me, sweetheart."

"Who are you talking to?" Annika asked from behind him.

"My wife," he replied without turning round. He felt Annika next to his shoulder.

"I shouldn't have interrupted you, I'm sorry," she said, quietly. "She was lucky to have a good man like you."

"I was the lucky one," he said, shaking his head.

"You were lucky to have each other," and said, diplomatically and touched his bare forearm, "and thank you for protecting my honour last night." They turned and walked back to the kitchen.

"Where is your husband buried?"

Her eyes looked like melting pools when tears began to build.

"Salisbury," then added, "I must travel there and visit his grave soon. It's been over a year now."

Angus changed the subject. "Do you know it's only two weeks until Christmas?"

She nodded and took a sip of her coffee. "What can I get for you as a gift?" she asked as she cupped the mug in her hands.

"there are no shops here," he replied, and left it at that.

Morton came into the kitchen without an ounce of regret.

"Mornin Angy, Annika." He nursed a black eye and purple bruising, where Angus's fist had connected. Fortunately, the radio sprang to life before an awkward conversation could happen.

"Station calling McLean."

Angus ran to the office picked up the radio. "Receiving."

"Postman's on his way," the voice on the radio told him."

"Copy that," Angus replied and placed the radio back on his desk again.

He met McGovern as he headed back to the kitchen and told him they were good to go. They had no baggage.

A short time later, a single helicopter landed, and Angus watched the two scouts board. As it took off a figure in the back waved at him, it was Van-Rooyen. Angus he waved back.

CHAPTER 15

*A*ngus tuned the radio in to RBC, and they listened to the news each night at nine. Three days later the news came on the presenter reported many Special Forces had raided a training camp inside Mozambique causing seriously heavy losses to the insurgents no reports of casualties in the Rhodesian force. When the announcer began reading cricket scores, he turned the radio off.

"That means we should get some peace. It should keep them quiet for a while."

Lindani agreed, "For now."

"How would you like to go to Salisbury and visit your husband's grave?" Angus asked Annika as they sat on the stoep a couple of days later.

"I can't travel there on my own," she replied, looking scared.

"I have to take the year end records to the department, tomorrow. You could come with me."

"I'd like that."

"Then it's a date." He said, playfully.

"Oh, now we're dating?" she asked, lifting her eyebrows.

No matter what Angus said, Annika managed to trap him at every turn.

When he opened his mouth to reply, she put a finger to his lips. "I'm toying with you."

The next day he gathered all his staff together and told them of their plans for the week.

Lindani was to take charge of the station while they were gone and asked if anyone had any problems he needed to deal with before he went. They all shook their heads.

The day came and Angus and Annika set off in the Isuzu. The staff waved goodbye from the front of the building. By mid-afternoon they had covered the one hundred and fifty kilometres and had reached the suburbs of Salisbury. Angus told her of his intention to take the records to the office the next morning, having booked them in to the George hotel in the centre of town.

"Booked us in?" she said, looking surprised, and he told her he'd booked two rooms for them.

When they arrived at the hotel, he parked the Isuzu in the parking lot. A bell boy came over and took both their overnight bags. Angus took out the two weapons he had brought with him: his R1 and one of the Argylls. At the reception desk he asked if he could put them in the gunroom. The receptionist told him only the manager had the keys. She called the manager to come to the desk and when he came; he led Angus to a strong room door that required both a combination lock and a key.

"Has sir checked the weapons are not loaded?" Angus nodded, placed the two weapons in a rack and thanked him.

Over dinner, he suggested Annika should go and visit her husband's grave while he was at the office. They arranged to go shopping once he had finished his meeting the following day.

When Annika had wine with her dinner, she commented

that she had almost forgotten the taste. Angus promised they would get some before heading back to Nyanga.

On his way to the office, he passed a jeweller's shop. He looked at the glittering array in the window and he spotted a little gold necklet with an oval emerald stone the size of a date attached. Angus went inside and bought it on impulse.

He arranged to meet up with Annika again at the hotel bar when they had both finished shopping. Later, when she walked into the bar, he could see she'd been crying. Her eyes were red rimmed.

"Are you okay?" he asked. She nodded and asked a waiter for a large glass of wine.

"Let's go shopping."

Three times they returned to the hotel that the afternoon, each time laden with bags full of items they had bought. There were Christmas gifts for the staff, and shirts of different styles and colours skirts for the women.

Angus bought a dozen glasses, so they wouldn't have to drink from the mugs all the time. Annika also bought at least a dozen different coloured vests. He told her they could finish their shopping the next morning, as now the shops were closing.

They met up again in the hotel lounge bar for a drink before dinner and she told him she had to go to the medical suppliers the following day as there were drugs, she didn't have and others she'd needed to top up for in the surgery. As they ate, Angus he told her he wanted to leave Salisbury by noon next day, so they could reach the station before dark.

After dinner they asked at the reception desk where the nearest cinema was the receptionist told them it was the Regal, but they would have to take a taxi as it was quite a distance from the hotel.

The taxi ride took five minutes through the bright lights of Salisbury, people going about their business. Everything normal before it drew up in front of the cinema; they joined the queue of people waiting to get in.

"We don't even know what they are showing," Angus said, laughing.

When they entered the foyer, the billboard showed it was a double bill; Clint Eastwood movie 'Dirty Harry' a B rated movie, starring Clint Eastwood and 'Tales from the Crypt' with Joan Collins.

They entered the semidarkness of the cinema as they went through the doors separating it from the foyer, they felt the coolness of the air-conditioning fresh on their faces. It felt wonderful after the heat they'd felt after ten minutes in the queue. The usherette showed them to their seats, and they settled as the lights dimmed in the cinema theatre and large red curtains parted.

The screen filled with a gold shield against a blue background. Both Angus and Annika sat in silence looking up at the screen eating popcorn they'd bought at the kiosk in the foyer.

When the first movie finished, a voice came over a loud-speaker to tell them there would be a brief interval. Usherettes came down each aisle with a tray that hung from her neck by a strap. They were selling ice cream in little cartons. Angus rose from his seat and bought one for each of them, it had been ages since he had tasted it.

The lights dimmed again as the red curtains parted; the screen came to life Pathe News all in black and white with various news stories from around the world, the trouping of the colour in London, Prime Minister Wilson meets Commonwealth leaders to discuss Rhodesian situation, Nixon being subpoenaed in the USA and Muhammad Ali knocks out Foreman in the eighth round.

The news reel finished, and the second movie started. It was a horror movie.

As he watched the storyline, Angus thought it was far-fetched.

Ordinary people would not put themselves in those situations.

Then it hit him. He was an ordinary man, yet he'd witnessed the horror in the workshop. He felt his eyes fill with tears, closed them, and tried to control his breathing. Bile rose to the back of his throat. He shook off his grief when she gripped his forearm tightly and buried her head on his chest to avoid the screen. A waft of perfume from her hair and her ponytail filled his senses.

"Are you Okay?" he whispered.

"I can't watch this," she confessed.

"Okay, let's get out of here." Standing, they made their way back to the brightly lit foyer.

When all the cabs passing were full, they began walking in the hotel's direction. It was still early when they reached its revolving door and felt the relief of the air-conditioning inside.

"Drink?" he asked.

"Just one," she replied. They sat in the lounge bar and Angus ordered brandy and coke for himself and a large white wine for Annika.

As they sipped the drinks, Angus told her he knew a land mine had killed her husband.

Where did it happen? he asked. He immediately felt annoyed with himself when he saw her eyes fill with tears.

We lived on the outskirts of Fort Victoria. Yannie was an accountant, a civil servant. He was traveling up here to Salisbury for a meeting when it happened. They killed him and three of his colleagues in the same car. Tears ran down her cheeks as she spoke, and Angus reached over and touched the back of her hand with his fingers.

"I'm sorry."

"Are you ready for bed," he asked when they'd finished their drinks. When Annika nodded, they headed upstairs. Walking her to her door, he said goodnight to her when they reached her door. Annika shook his hand, thanked him for the evening and kissed his cheek. Angus's face flushed, and he hurried down the corridor to the safety of his room.

The following morning, they had a full breakfast in the restaurant with orange juice and coffee knowing it would be all they would get to eat until they reached Nyanga later in the day. Angus drove them out of the parking lot, with all their purchases from the previous day's expedition loaded into the caged back of the Izuzu and headed for the department supplies store. There Annika got the drugs and other items she needed for the surgery.

When they'd finished, Angus drove across the town, stopping outside a bottle store. After checking what Annika's favorite wine was, he told her to wait in the truck while he went into the store.

"Five cases of Castle lager, please."

"Only got Elephant because of the sanctions. None of the other bottle stores can get any from the suppliers either."

When Angus agreed to take Elephant and asked for five cases, he was told, "only two per customer." he said. The store manager told his assistant to put two cases on his trolley.

"Anything else?" he asked. Four cases of Klipdrift. Again, the store hand shook his head.

"Any brand of brandy? "Angus asked.

"Yes, Klipdrift, but only one case per customer." Fuck.

Angus thought was this guy deliberately trying to ruin his day.

"Okay, and four cases of Kamala white.

"Only two per customer." The store hand was really irritating him now.

"fuck it, okay two." He paid the man, and his assistant took his trolley to the truck. He told her of the pantomime in the bottle store and she laughed. They drove to another bottle store only to get the same performance there, he had to visit four in total to get everything he wanted.

When fully laden with their supplies, he pointed the truck eastward, relieved to be heading back at last, and it was comfortable in the cab with the air-conditioning running. The journey passed as they discussed everything they'd needed to do back at the station.

They had only gone forty kilometres when a wrecked car came into sight, further up the road. It lay shattered on its roof. Angus knew it hadn't been there the day before. Reaching behind him, he took down his R1, laid across his lap, then placed the Argyle on the middle seat beside him. Annika looked anxious.

"What's happened?"

"No idea, but I have a feeling we're about to find out. Angus didn't slow down as he skirted the crater in the road and the remains of a Ford Fairlane, its underneath now pointing to the sky, was concave and burned out.

"Landmine," he said as he watched the wreck grow smaller in the rearview mirror. Annika's eyes filled with tears when she turned and looked at him. "That could have been us, Angus. We only came down this road yesterday."

Annika said nothing else during the journey, and eventually they made it onto the dirt track road that led to the station. Angus stopped short of the rise in the road as he had before. He took his binoculars from the dash, praying they would not be presented with what he'd seen the last time he'd come back.

When he got out of the truck, she asked him what was wrong. Angus told her to wait in the truck and made his way to where he had an excellent view of the station. He lifted his binoculars to his eyes with trepidation. With his heart pumping, he focused on the camp and zoomed the lens for a closer look. A wave of relief swept over him when he saw Lindani and the others, they were gathered around two Crocodile Transporters.

Angus ran back to the truck.

"It's alright over and over as he climbed into the cab and pushed the gear lever into first gear.

"What's alright, Angus?" she asked.

When Angus relived what he found the last time he had viewed the camp from there, she put her hand out, stroked the side of his face, and gave a sympathetic smile.

Seeing them enter the compound, the others left the Crocodile transporters and gathered around the truck. Angus and Annika climbed down.

"Park the truck around the back near the kitchen door, Manodno and to get help to unload it."

The guys who had delivered the crocs showed him how everything worked he pointed to the co-axel machine guns on top.

"What are those?" Angus asked, pointing at the arms.

"Browning .50 calibre gun. They work in tandem. They're angled slightly so when they're fired, they hit the target eighty millimetres apart to give you bigger spread," one of the drivers told him. Use them sparingly, there's only four, five hundred round boxes of ammunition spare, and the two boxes already mounted by the guns. Go careful if you use it, they fire five hundred rounds a minute."

The two men said they couldn't spend the night as they were picking up a patrol nearby. Shortly afterwards, they shook hands and were quickly on their way.

CHAPTER 16

$\mathcal{L}$indani told Angus there was nothing to report and Angus clapped him on the shoulder in appreciation. After dinner Angus sat on the stoep with Annika and Lindani, telling him about their trip. When they'd finished Lindani got to his feet and began fidgeting.

"What's wrong?" Angus said, picking up on Lindani's vibe.

Lindani cleared his throat. "Would it be okay for me to go home?"

"For good?" Angus asked, stunned.

Ignoring Angus's question, he continued. "Dzingia wants to go as well. He comes from my village."

"For good?" Angus asked, alarmed, his brow furrowed and his mind in chaos.

Landani shook his head. "It's been a year since we last visited our homes."

"Oh! Of course, you can," he gushed, his voice laced with relief they'd only wanted to visit.

"When do you want to go?"

Lindani hesitated. "We would like to visit at Christmas." Angus felt shocked they hadn't mentioned this sooner.

"Christmas is only two days away. Take one of the Land Rovers. Get your things ready and leave for home tomorrow."

"Lindani, I have told you many times before, not only do you work for me, but you're also my friend… my best friend." Angus clapped him on the back and Landani grinned. "I must tell Dzingia" as he left the stoep.

Angus and Annika stood at the rail, watching as he ran to the workshop.

"Those two would be hard to replace," he murmured.

Annika placed her hand on his shoulder in an intimate gesture and looked up at him. "You're a good man," she said, remaining there at his side with a hand on his shoulder.

He felt awkward and shy at the gesture and didn't move. When let her hand slip from his shoulder, he breathed a sigh of relief, because he'd almost reacted to her touch by placing his hand on hers. Moving away, he sat down. When came and sat down next to him, he was stuck for something to say.

"Last night was the first time I'd been to the cinema since I came to Rhodesia, in fact it was only the second time I've been to the cinema." Annika looked surprised and raised her eyebrows. "The only other time was the night before Morag, and I flew to Heathrow from Glasgow."

"There was no cinema near where you lived?"

"No, I told you I come from a very rural village. It was so remote; the only entertainment was ceilidh every two months in the church hall."

"What is that?"

"A ceilidh? It's Gaelic, meaning dance.

"What's Gaelic?"

"A Scottish language."

Annika looked puzzled. "And you speak this language?" he shook his head.

"When you were wooing you wife, where did you go, what did you do?"

Angus told her he met her at school she was two years older than him, and when he returned from university, he asked her father if he could start seeing her.

"You asked her father if you could see her?" he nodded. She put her hand over her mouth to hide a smile. Angus knew it seemed old-fashioned.

"I am sorry Angus, but that seems very ancient." She leaned into him and hugged his bicep for a few seconds before letting go again. "So, what did you do with your wife when you took her out?"

He shrugged his shoulders. "Go for walks when the weather was fine." she shook her head "that does not seem like much of a courtship?"

He shrugged again "it was all we had."

After a few moments, she said, "My boyfriends would take me to the cinema or dancing most weekends."

"Boyfriends?" he quizzed.

She nodded and chuckled. "Only one at a time."

The way she looked at him, he knew he'd pushed himself into yet another corner. Silence fell between them until Annika probed farther.

"Come on Angus, we're both adults, there's no need to be embarrassed."

"What do you mean?"

"We're good friends now and should be able to talk freely," she explained, gently.

He told her how he felt although he kept putting keeping his foot in his mouth and didn't know how to read her.

"What way would you like to take me?" she asked in a flirty tone.

"There you go again," he replied, feeling vindicated. He immediately felt embarrassed at the innuendo. He knew he had to break this conversation off before he made a complete arse of himself. "Right, I'm off to bed it's been a long day. Goodnight." As he turned to go, he heard her reply.

"Goodnight, Angus."

He woke early next morning, Lindani and Dzingia had been bouncing about the hall for hours.

"What time can we go Angoos?"

"You might as well have gone last night. I could have got some sleep then," he said, letting him know they had awoken him early. Angus poured himself a cup of coffee from the pot on the ranging.

"I'll take the patrol today. You can you tell the others," he advised, Landani.

This was his escape route from Annika. At least he wouldn't have to face her again all day.

As daylight broke, they set out on patrol. Angus drove the big Crocodile, Manodno on the heavy machine gun on its top. Landani drove the Isuzu, Chatambuza stayed behind in the station.

They were gone longer than usual but never too far from the station, returning just as it got dark. When Angus parked up at the side of the main building, Annika strode over to him.

"What took you so long? I was getting worried."

Angus excused himself, telling her it had been a long day. All he wanted was a shower, something to eat and his bed. While the kitchen was empty, he grabbed a bottle of brandy and quickly took it to his room, knowing it would be a long night in there himself.

Shit, I'm becoming a prisoner on my own station.

As soon as he'd finished eating, he said goodnight to everyone at the table and went to his room. He spread out on his sofa and sipped at the brandy. He had drunk almost half of the bottle by the time he eventually fell onto his bed.

On Christmas eve, Angus woke early. He'd told himself the night before he was not going to hide from Annika that day and would stand up to her better. He wondered if that had been the brandy speaking and whether he'd have the courage to do this.

He noted Dova and Busani had the fire pit going; Banele was hanging the meat on the spit; Impala sirloin and two whole small piglets. There was enough cooked meat cooking so as no one would have to cook Christmas day.

The smell of fresh bread from the oven filled the air and the festive season appeared to touch everyone. Even his tormentor had left him alone and pleasant towards him. With no patrol that day, they all did little jobs around the compound. By sunset, everything was in order. The stoep table had been set, laid out with the meat, potatoes, rice, tomatoes, and a big bowl of fresh fruits. When they all arrived on the stoep they tucked in, Dove had put a bottle of brandy on the table and bottles of beer in a tub filled with ice. A bottle of Annika's Kamala also sat on top with condensation glistening on the bottle.

They had a long meal then as they drifted away when Dova and Busani cleared the table, they sat alone on the stoep. Angus felt the same uneasiness around Annika. She was on her second bottle of wine; she got up and went indoors, when she came over to him stooped and kissed him on the cheek.

"Happy Christmas," she said, handing him a small package.

"In the Netherlands we exchange them this evening." He told her in Scotland they did not exchange gifts until Christmas day.

"I can't take this," he protested, shocked when he opened it. It was a watch, a Rolex Watch. "Where did you get it?"

"It was my wedding gift to Yannie," she smiled, but it was a sad smile.

"Then you keep it as a memento." She shook her head. "I have no use for it now."

He got up and went indoors and he gave her the little box on his return.

"Oh, Angus it's beautiful." Angus felt pleased she liked it and told her he'd picked it up when they'd been in Salisbury.

"It reminded me of your eyes." As soon as the words were out, he'd felt awkward again and stared at the floor. When he looked back up, she was smiling.

"It really is lovely, Angus." She passed him the chain from the box and turned around. "Would you put it on for me?"

He looped his arms over her head to hold the chain ends in each hand; she reached and lifted her ponytail exposing the back of her neck. As Angus fumbled, thinking he'd never manage the tiny clasp, his fingers brushed the soft skin on the back of her neck.

"There," he said when he'd fastened it on the second try.

Annika ran inside, leaving Angus convinced he'd done something wrong until she came back with a wide smile on her face. His eyes flitted to her lips, then back to her gaze.

"And?" she asked.

Angus looked puzzled. "and what?"

Annika lifted the stone from her chest. "Does it still remind you of my eyes?"

Angus stared at her eyes. They were more intense than the stone. "Yes" he admitted, awkwardly.

"I have a special outfit to wear for Christmas, would you tell me if you like it?" She left him sitting on the stoep, wondering why what he thought should matter.

When she hadn't come back ten minutes later, he went inside to find her. Her bedroom door was closed. He stood for a moment, wondering if he should knock. But decided against it. Instead, he went and closed the front door and went to his room. When he sat on the sofa, he poured another brandy from the bottle he'd sneaked in there the night before. He leaned back with his face pointing to the ceiling.

After a few minutes, he straightened up to take another drink and noticed a chink of light coming from under the door leading to his bed. He stood, walked over, and opened it.

Annika was lying naked on top of his bed, her blonde hair loose from the ponytail spread over the white pillows which contrasted with her tanned body. The green stone rested between her breasts.

"Do you like my outfit, Angus?" he froze, then closed the door quickly. Seconds later the door flew open, and Annika stood, still naked, in front of him. "Angus McLean, get in here now." He stood rooted to the spot, unsure what to do.

"I'm your real Christmas gift and you are mine," she said with a wicked grin. She grabbed the front of his shirt and pulled him into the room.

"Listen, you have had quite a lot to drink," he protested. Annika shook her head and kissed him on the mouth, her tongue slipping into his mouth.

She led him toward the bed. "Now" she said in a seductive tone. "get these off." Her finger waved up and down his body, toward his clothing.

"I have to go to the bathroom,", he said, excusing himself, and walked into the en-suite. He took his clothes off and freshened up. When he came back, she was lying on his bed propped up on one elbow.

Dressed in only boxer shorts, Angus walked over to the bed. He moved to switch the light off.

"Leave it on," she said, moving quickly from the bed and pulled his shorts to his ankles. "I meant all of them off," she said with a grin. "There, I've seen you naked now." Annika pulled him on to the bed. "I've wanted to do this since I met you," she confessed, leaned in, and kissed him, her tongue exploring his mouth. Angus was only a man and his restraint only went so far, so he began exploring hers in return. She felt so warm, her fingers stroking his chest, he began stroking her sides.

Taking his hand, she placed it over her breast. Angus felt he her nipple stiffen against the cupped palm of his hand. He dipped his head and took it in to his mouth, rolling her other nipple gently with his other hand. She threw her head back and let out a moan.

Trailing her fingers across his stomach, her hand drifted lower and lower. She touched his erect cock, and it sent a shudder of desire straight through him.

Angus gently traced a line down the middle of her flat stomach. Her skin felt like silk. At her navel she gave a little twitch and drew a deep breath. He continued down to the hair on her mound, and it felt soft. Annika reached down and took one of his fingers and guided it to her clitoris.

"Touch me here," she instructed. He immediately began rubbing gently, then his finger moved on down between her thighs until he felt her wetness. "Oh," she gasped, digging her nails in to his shoulder as he slipped a finger inside her. Inserting another, he drew them in and out. "That's not what I want. I need to feel you inside me," she whispered as she pulled him on top of her, gripping his stiff erection and guiding his cock inside her.

Angus groaned at the sensation of her all around him. It had been a while since he'd felt consumed by a woman's body. As he slipped out and in, she bit hard on his shoulder until the tension built within her and her body convulsed.

She let out a groan, and cried his name, "Angus." Hearing her reaction, he couldn't hold back any longer and as he came, the feeling shook his body as he filled her.

They both lay in silence, panting and sweating. Quietly he lay on his back, eyes closed as he caught his breath, and his heartbeat was just beginning to slow down to normal. He felt her move on the bed then touch his cock again. It stiffened, and he opened his eyes as she moved down the bed and took him into her mouth.

Angus tried to sit up. "What are you doing?"

"Shhh" she said, pushing him down and continued, sliding his cock in and out of her lips. The heat of her mouth drove him crazy, and it wasn't long again before he came. As he did, he tried to pull away, but she gripped his throbbing shaft firmly until he could feel his juice pulse as it flowed from him. "Mmmm, now we have no secrets, and we're not friends, we're lovers," she said, ss Angus lay drained.

They slept in each other's arms until early morning. It was still dark when Angus explored and rubbed her clitoris.

"Mmmm," she murmured. "Good morning. Are you going to give me another gift?" Angus had needed no further encouragement. They made love twice; long and slow now that the initial animal passion had passed.

When they heard movement in the corridor. He jumped from the bed. "Shit, the others are up, what are we going to do?"

Annika sat naked in the bed, laughing.

"Shhh" he said, with his finger to his lips.

"Angus, we're adults." he looked confused. "What if they find out?" his eyes going from the door to the window looking for an escape route. This caused her to laugh until tears flowed down her cheeks as she sat with her hands clasped over her legs, her knees at her chin.

A knock came on the bedroom door "Oh fuck," Angus mumbled.

"Come in," she shouted. Dova opened the door and came in with a tray with two cups of coffee. When Angus tried to cover himself, both the women laughed.

He ran to the bathroom, leaving the two women in hysterics in his.

"Your coffee's getting cold," Annika shouted when Dove had gone. When Angus reappeared, he was wearing shorts. "Angus, calm down." He knew how it must have looked to her, but his face was scarlet.

"How the fuck did she know you were in here?" he asked, then his face looked even more shocked. "She saw me naked."

"It was probably women's intuition and when you saw her half naked, you said it was their way, so I'm sure she doesn't mind." She chuckled. "Angus, we'll be spending a lot of time together I have l am going to take great pleasure in showing how to be happy."

When they were dressed, they went to the stoep. It was like the walk of shame when he saw they were all there. He felt his face redden again, but no one seemed to take notice. Dova and Busani were admiring Annika's necklet.

"Angus the presents." Annika prompted.

"Oh yes," he said, happy to get off that stoep.

He came back and handed the presents to Annika for the women, and he handed the men theirs while she handed hers to the women. They all opened the packages and got busy showing each other what they had been given.

"See?" Annika said, "no one cares what we do." She stuck her tongue out at him and smiled. Glancing towards the others, he agreed and began to feel more confident in her company; they went and inspected the animals in the pens and surgery.

"Angus you had to kill men a few months ago how did it affect you?" she asked as they walked around the compound.

He frowned, wondering why she'd bring up. "Why do you ask?"

Annika drew a breath. "In case I ever have to do it."

Angus thought for a moment. "It's a sickening feeling but, if you or your friends are in danger you don't think about it." She just nodded, and they fell silent again for a while.

"Last night was the first time you had oral sex?" she suddenly asked. He was thrown off balance by her question, and he felt himself blush. "Have you ever done it to a woman?"

"What is this game you're playing?"

Annika gave him a hard stare. "Angus, I am not playing any games with you I'm attracted to you," she told him. "I have been trying to attract your attention since I got here, but you always back away. I thought you weren't ready for a relationship."

"And I thought you were toying with me." They both laughed until she leaned in and pressed her lips to his. He kissed her long, deep, and passionate, it had been so long since he'd tasted a kiss.

He broke the kiss as he heard clapping and whistles coming from the building. They turned and saw they had all been watching them. Fuck it, he thought and kissed her again, then waved in their direction with his arm wrapped around Annika's waist.

When they arrived on the stoep, they all congratulated the couple. Early that afternoon Dova came and asked if they could go to the workshop early as they wished to spend a traditional African Christmas.

Angus nodded. "Yes, you enjoy yourselves."

Annika gave him a look of disappointed which confused Angus as he'd agreed.

Annika tugged at his T-shirt. "That was a hint they were giving us space."

"Was it?"

She shook her head, like she couldn't believe now naïve he was and chuckled. "Yes. Come to the bedroom now."

"But it's the afternoon," he protested.

"I can see that, but I want you again," she whispered, seductively.

By the time they turned up for dinner, Angus was of the opinion she was insatiable. After they'd eaten, Dova came to them and informed them she'd moved Annika's things into Angus's room. When he didn't react, Annika thought they were getting somewhere and smiled.

They went to the workshop to listen to the others sing Acapello which was a joy to hear. Angus and Annika joined in clapping along to the African music. It was late by the time they went back to the main building.

"I think I might do a patrol tomorrow," Angus told Annika.

"No, you can't, not tomorrow, its Boxing Day." he had forgotten. They went straight to his bedroom and got ready for bed. When he came out of the bathroom, he was wearing boxer shorts and a bright blue T-shirt.

"Off," Annika said, wagging her finger at his attire. Angus said nothing but stripped as she asked.

He switched the light off and paused when she didn't protest that he had; he climbed into bed. They lay in the darkness, her head on his chest, and sighed.

"Annika, what happens to you when we make love?"

She lifted her head from his chest. "What do you mean 'happens'?"

"You shook really badly as we finished."

She smiled in the darkness "I was having an orgasm, Angus."

"You really are an innocent. Didn't your wife never have them?"

"Morag didn't enjoy lovemaking, she just thought it was a wife's duty. She'd never have put my penis in her mouth." He went on to tell her they'd only made love around twice or three times a month, always in the dark, with Morag underneath him.

"You only ever had sex in one position?"

His chest felt tight at her questions, but he nodded his head and mumbled his confirmation in the dark.

"You poor thing Angus we are going to correct that aren't we?" no answer came his breath slowed as his fell asleep.

CHAPTER 17

The day after Boxing Day, Angus took out a small patrol using the crocodile only and came back before noon. He was on the stoep when he heard a car horn in the distance, he looked in the direction a cloud of dust was rising it came in to view it was the Land Rover Lindani was driving, the front seat empty, in the back was a woman, she was bending over something.

"Dzingia has been shot!" Lindani shouted as he brought the vehicle to a stop in a cloud of dust.

When Angus ran over Dzingia was a mass of blood. "Get him to the surgery," he ordered, and Landani drove the extra meters before he and Lindani carried their friend inside. Lying him on the examining table, Angus ripped Dzingia's shirt open as Annika came with a bowl of sterile water and antiseptic. Dabbing the wound with a large swab, she cleared away the blood enough to see two exit wounds and knew he'd been he shot twice from the back. His intestines spilled from his stomach, and between them the two holes were as big as a fist.

"I'll do what I can, but he's going need to get to a surgeon to operate if he's going to survive," she said solemnly as she rushed to a drawer and came back with a rubber tube with a bulb hand pump in the centre of the tube. "Give me that bowl," she ordered, nodding at the bowl of water.

Lindani passed it to her she put I on the floor next to the examination table she put one end of the tube in a wound and let the other end fall in the bowl. When she began to pump, she told them he'd been hit in the large bowel. The stench of faeces and urine hung in the air and a few squeezes of the ball, they saw yellow and green discharge mixed with blood taint the water. She bent her head then looked sadly towards Angus as Dzingia began to moan in pain.

Angus ran to the Land Rover and brought back the medicine box. He handed Annika a small ampule pen of morphine and she immediately stick it into a vein.

While Annika worked on cleaning the wounds, he called for Manodno to bring a cot from the workshop, and when he arrived back with it, they lifted Dzingia from the table and told them to take him to the house.

"No, he'd be better here, it's a sterile environment," Annika protested.

"Where did this happen?" he asked, Lindani.

"Where the game path crossed the road to the station. Dzingia was standing in the back holding on to the roll bar and we had past the game path when it happened.

"Right, Manodno stay here for security. Get the dogs, Landani. We're going out to find them."

He turned to Annika. "If anything happens when we're away, Manodno will bring the others in here," he replied, agreeing not to move Dzingia.

He kissed her on the forehead, headed to the Crocodile and left the compound in the direction they had come. Lindani drove while Angus manned the machine guns on top. Mandala and Chatambuza sat opposite each other scrutinizing the left and right through the firing slots on the sloped sides.

They passed the game trail but did not stop Angus shouted to Lindani above the roar of the engine he had missed it, Mandala stuck his head through the turret opening he says the path leads to the river he was going around.

He stopped short of the riverbed, there was only a trickle of water in the middle, it hadn't rained for two weeks. Angus knew it would only need one overnight storm to bring it in to flood again. They headed upriver and stopped the crocodile three hundred meters nearer to where the trail and the river merged. He shut the engine down and waited.

"Make sure we get them all in the out in the open," he whispered to the others. They crept closer to where the trail emerged.

When the insurgents came into view from the brush and piled onto to the sandy riverbed, Angus and his men snapped the safety catches off and instantly rapid fired. The insurgents had no time to react and in seconds all eight of them lay dead. They swooped in and took their weapons away.

"Where does this one come from? Lindani asked pointing to the corpses.

"Korean or Chinese?" Angus said as he bent down and took a camera from the bag attached to dead man's waist.

Once back at the compound, Mandala opened the gate and Angus headed straight to the surgery, where he knew Annika would still be with Dzingia.

"How is he?" Angus asked, his face etched with anguish.

"He won't live," she said, solemnly.

"I'll stay with him," he replied, decisively.

"I'll as well. Did you manage to find the guys who did this?"

"All dead," he responded, rubbed his hand through his hair and stared down at poor Dzingia.

Annika moved toward him and hugged him tight.

"Do you know what? I don't feel sorry at all."

Angus blinked back tears, bent over Dzingia kissed his forehead and straightened up, turning to look at Annika tears rolled down his cheeks. "Dinner is ready," Dova said interrupting them quietly from the surgery door.

Angus shook his head. "go and get something to eat," he encouraged Annika. Sensing he wanted time alone Annika did as he asked, leaving him silently weeping as Dzingia clung to life.

Lindani stealthily came shoulder to shoulder with Angus, he hadn't heard him come in.

"We share our grief again Angoos."

Both men sat in silence until Annika came back and Lindani stood taller.

"I must go to see my wife." He said and left them alone in the surgery.

"This is affecting him, greatly," Angus said, "his wife is lying beside Morag."

"He brought another woman back with him, isn't she his wife?" Angus had forgotten the woman tending to Dzingia.

"Anashe, the woman he brought back with him, said she's Landani's is his wife," she told him.

This was news to Angus, but he stayed silent, walked to the cabinet where the linens were kept and pulled out a mosquito net. They rigged it up over the cot Dzingia lay on to keep the flies off him, and just as they finished Lindani came back with another two cots.

"How is he doing?" Both Angus and Annika shook their heads.

After setting up the cots, they sat in silence, the only light in the room being the blue glare of the electric fly killer.

Dzingia began to moan again, and Angus stood, drew up a shot of morphine and quietened him down. Once he had settled both he and Annika stretched out on the cots and fell asleep late in the night.

He had no idea how long he'd slept when Annika gave him a gentle shake and he opened his eyes with a start.

"He's gone," she whispered, sniffing quietly.

They left his body in the surgery and walked across the moon light path to the main building. Angus headed straight to the pantry and brought out a bottle of brandy. Pouring a third of the bottle into a mug, he swallowed most of it in greedy burning gulps.

Annika had been about to remind him he hadn't eaten, then thought better of it.

"I'm going to bed," she whispered instead. She lay staring at the ceiling and struggled to sleep; it was the first time she'd had to watch a man die.

When she woke the following morning, Angus had not come to bed. Rising off the bed, she looked in the bathroom, but he wasn't there. When she passed Dova, she told her she had found him slumped on the kitchen table. He'd woken up but told Dova he hadn't wanted to disturb Annika.

She found him sitting on the stoep and went and sat beside him. Tension rolled off his body and he banged his fist on the table. "This is my fault. I shouldn't have let them go."

"Don't blame yourself," she admonished, reaching out and touching the back of his hand.

Lindani saw Angus's outburst and came onto the stoep. Angus broke the news about Dzingia and was surprised when Landani's huge brown eyes welled up as he struggled to hold back the tears.

"I'll dig his grave," Lindani stated.

"I'll help you," Angus agreed.

Annika couldn't bring herself to go over to the surgery,

not with the body there. She sat on the stoep and wondered how they could have been so happy yesterday morning when today was very different. Eventually all the women in the station came out and joined her, they sat in silence mourning their friend.

When they'd finished their preparations, Angus and Landani went into the surgery. Minutes later they came to tell everyone they were ready to bury Dzingia. When they, all went to the makeshift graveyard, they took Dzingia's body wrapped in his sleeping blanket; and placed him in the open grave.

Angus tried his best to conduct the sermon talking about the time he knew Dzingia, but when his words began to dry up Lindani began to sing the twenty third psalm, 'The Lords My Shepherd'. They all joined in and Angus suddenly remembered they had mostly been educated by missionaries. When the burial was over the others left Angus and Lindani alone. Without speaking, they filled filled in the grave with the red acrid dry soil.

No one worked that day, taking their time to mourn the loss of Dzingia.

"How many men were involved?" she asked, and Angus knew immediately she meant those who'd attacked Dzingia.

"Eight," he replied, deadpan.

"You killed them all?" Angus didn't reply but his ashen face told her they had.

"What about their bodies?"

"Hyena's, vultures or some other predatory animal will have found them by now."

"Oh! Angus, how could you do that?" she asked, clearly shocked by this callous act.

He banged the table with his fist again and she jumped. "You saw what they did to Dzingia what others did to my wife and the others in the graveyard. We've been too complacent here recently. We tend to forget there's war going on around us."

Angus called for Lindani and when he came into view, he asked him to go and ask Banele and Dakaria, the two new men in the station if them if either of them could shoot. When the answer was no Angus looked frustrated.

"Tomorrow Mandala and Manodno must teach them how to use the AK47s. Take the Crocodile with you. You can drive and stand guard over them with the Brownings. From now on two men will be on watch every night, one in the building and one in the workshop."

Lindani turned to leave. "Annika says you have brought a wife here?" It was more of a question than a statement. Lindani nodded. "Three days and you come back with a new wife?"

Lindani nodded again. "My brother went to gather wood for the fire after my last visit. He didn't return, some say he was killed, so now his wife is mine."

Africa! Angus thought Africa would he never figure it out?

"Her name is Anashe."

"Then I would like to meet her" Angus said. He brought back a very young beautiful woman wearing a burnt orange sundress. She was looked much younger than Lindani. From the way she looked to the ground Angus saw she was shy and self-conscious.

"Hi, I'm Angus, and this is Annika."

Aneshe gave a little bend of her knees. "I am very happy to meet you, Bwana and you Missey."

"No, you will call us Angus and Annika. We don't have Bwanas or Missys here, only friends.

Her face broke into a huge grin. "Yes, Bwana."

He pointed to his chest and scowled. "Angus." Lindani led

her   away.

Everybody was in a grave mood after Dzingia's passing and when they had finished dinner, he went in doors with Lindani and brought bottles of brandy, beer, and wine. They put them on the table. He poured drinks and passed them out.

"To Dzingia," he said and held his glass up to toast his passing. Lindani and Manodno poured another. Lindani said the same in Shona, and after the toast they all drifted away.

"Do you want to go to bed? Annika asked.

"You go on I will be in soon."

"Don't sit up drinking again tonight Angus." He sat alone in silence for a while and eventually got up and headed indoors.

The bedroom door was open, and the lamp was out. He began taking his clothes off in the darkness.

"Shorts and T-shirt" she said.

When he lay down beside her, he put his arm across her waist she had a tank top on. They drifted off to sleep his body following the contours of hers.

The following morning Lindani had everything they needed already loaded into the Crocodile. Angus told him to keep in touch by radio the radio in the Crocodile. It had been built for military use, so he assumed the handsets had a wider range with its long whip Ariel.

He stood watching as they headed out making a large dust cloud before vanishing into the bush. Lindani had informed him they were heading for the Ugura riverbed.

The mood in the station was still incredibly low. He had gone with Annika to the holding pens earlier while she'd looked at animals. The Wildebeest calf was growing fast and was now eating foliage. Annika said he could be released anytime a herd was close by before they started heading north with the rains, and the cheetah could go within a few days.

He sat on the stoep steps the RPD sat on its tripod next to him. Clouds were in the sky.

"Hopefully, we'll get more rain today." It had not rained for two weeks, only electrical storms with their spectacular light shows, but no rain to accompany them.

Dova had served him some fruit and a glass of iced tea when the sun had just peaked in the sky. The clouds had started build but came to nothing. Eventually, the Crocodile came lumbering back to the compound and when it stopped Angus asked how they had done. Lindani told him Dakaria would be ok with a few more sessions, but he felt that Banele couldn't have made dust rise if he fired the bullets directly toward the ground.

Angus said they could go out again the day after tomorrow as the next day was New Year's Day and everyone should rest. They sat on the stoep that night eating and drinking, the atmosphere felt lighter than the days before, helped by the fact he had opened the office window and the radio played loud enough they heard it on the stoep.

Still the rain that had threatened hadn't fell, leaving a balmy night with broken cloud in the sky. The three-quarter moon gave off silver edges as most of the others drifted away until only, he and Annika remained.

The radio presenter was describing celebrations for countries in different time zones; numerous functions were being attended by named dignitaries they'd heard of in Bulawayo, Fort Victoria and Salisbury as the New Year dawned upon them.

As mid-night struck the radio played a recording of Big Ben striking twelve and the solemn voice of the presenter announced, "Welcome to nineteen seventy-seven."

Angus leaned in and kissed Annika, pulled back and smiled "Happy New Year love. Let's hope it is a good one."

"I know this will be a good year, the first of many, now I have you," she replied, staring intently into his eyes before she kissed him back.

"Everyone at the Rhodesian Broadcasting Corporation would like to wish you all happiness and prosperity for nineteen seventy-seven. We will resume broadcasting at seven thirty this morning," the radio announcer said before the radio program went dead.

Angus stood, went into his office, turned the radio off and closed the window. Annika was still sitting on the stoop when he went back out. "Bed?"

"Yes please," she replied, stretching her arms lazily above her head.

They were lying on the bed in the dark when he felt her hand touch his penis. Angus turned on his side to face her, but Annika pushed him onto his back, got up and straddled him above his waist. She leant forward and kissed him, her long silky hair brushing his chest as their tongues tangled and tasted one another.

"Do remember what you said after that first night we spent together?" he asked when they had broken the kiss.

She drew back a little and looked at him, puzzled. "When you asked if I'd ever performed oral sex on a woman?"

"Yes," he paused, "I wouldn't know how."

Mmmm, she hummed. "Do want me to teach you?" he nodded. "Slide down the bed a little."

Angus did as he asked and she positioned herself astride his head above his shoulders, facing down his body. Lowering herself to his face she said, "Use your tongue the way you would use a finger." As he tentatively explored her sex with his tongue, he felt her breath on his shaft right before she enveloped it into her mouth.

They lay locked together until she began to shake and moaned around his length still in her mouth. As her orgasm tore through her he held her buttocks tight, his fingers blanching her skin in his effort to stop her escaping as she squirmed. What they did had so erotic he couldn't hold back, and his own explosive orgasm made him empty into her mouth.

She rolled off and lay down beside him. Neither of them said anything, their heavy breathing the only sound cutting into the silence in the dark.

"Did I do it properly?"

Annika rose on an elbow and kissed him on the cheek.

"Only…" she began

"Only what?" he asked.

"Only too properly," he breathed a sigh of relief.

Angus took her into him, his arm behind her neck.

"Too properly?"

"Yeah polite, but if that's you holding back then I can't wait until you let go.

He smiled. "That's that problem solved."

"What did you think?" she asked.

He grinned in the dark. "What else have I been missing? That was mind blowing."

Annika sat up and got off the bed. "Do you want me to show you?"

He nodded in the dark, and she switched on the light. She knelt back on the bed on all fours. "Come to me and enter behind me, Angus." as he did, she reached between her open legs and slid him inside her. "Same as you did on top" her face sunk to the pillow he thrust in and out gathering pace as she opposed him. She convulsed as he exploded inside her, he thought his insides were trying about to leave his body through his penis. He collapsed his head resting on her back. "Happy New Year" she said "definitely" he replied they fell asleep in each other's arms. Next morning Lindani had the Crocodile ready again to take Dakaria and Banele out again, he told Lindani to concentrate on Dakaria and to try Banele with an Argyle and an RPD.

He spent the day pretty much the same way they went out on New Year's Eve sitting on the steps with the other RPD close to him.

CHAPTER 18

Mid-afternoon the Crocodile came lumbering up to the gates again, came into the compound and stopped next to the steps. The tailgates opened and men jumped down and when McGovern appeared. Oh! No not another night with Morton, was Angus's first thoughts were, but McGovern was alone and looked in a terrible state. He looked exhausted, his hair matted and flattened as his red rimmed eyes looked out from his red dust encrusted face. Angus led him to the stoep where McGovern flopped onto a chair.

Dova poured tea from the jug into an enamel mug and handed it to him. Angus waited as he swallowed the tea greedily then held out the mug for a refill, eventually slowing down.

"Where are you going? What's happened?" Angus asked.

"I need to be picked up by air support."

"That daft wee shite would never listen" he blurted, confusing Angus.

"Who?"

"Morton he's only gone and got himself killed."

"Shot?" Angus asked sounding alarmed.

McGovern shook his head. "Just killed."

He went on to tell him they'd settled in two Acacia trees to bivouac for the night, like they usually did on patrol, the trees were about fifty meters apart.

"Morton signalled he'd spotted something in the brush, he'd signalled for me to wait it out, but the next thing he jumped down from the tree and closed in on the brush. He vanished from view for a few seconds then came back flying through the air, followed by a big Warthog Boar who gored him," he shut his eyes at the memory. "It took four rounds to bring it down."

"Oh, my, God," Angus said, horrified.

McGovern nodded. "By the time I got down to him he was still alive but bleeding heavily. A tusk had penetrated the femoral artery in his groin. I tried to stem the flow, but he bled out ten minutes later." He spread his hands on the table. "I had to sit it out overnight in the Acacia, listening to the hyenas and wild dogs scrapping over his body." he fell silent for a moment before speaking again. "I had to use what water we had to wash his blood off so I wouldn't become quarry.

Angus observed him closer and saw dried blood beneath his nails. "Come on, get in the shower." He led him to what had been Annika's room after instructing Dova to take him some soap and a towel.

Fifteen minutes later he came back to the stoep a while later.

"I needed that. I feel nearly human again," he said.

"Do you need to use the radio to call it in?"

"Can I leave it until later, I'm exhausted. They can pick me up in the morning. We're expecting a build-up in activities, you need to be careful." Angus nodded.

"We lost one of our men two days ago," Angus confessed, "we buried him yesterday."

"Where did that happen?" McGovern asked.

"South of here, about eight kilometers away. We went in pursuit of them," Angus told him.

"Did you find them?" Angus nodded.

"How many?"

"Eight." McGovern's eyes widened.

"You got them?"

Angus nodded, briefly reliving the moment. "One of them was Korean or something."

"Did you get any maps or anything," McGovern asked.

"A camera… we got a camera," he told him, suddenly remembering it.

"Can I see it?"

"Sure, it's still the Crocodile," he said, standing.

Angus fetched the camera from the cab of the vehicle and passed it to him.

"This isn't a camera it's a starlight scope," McGovern said, turning the object over in his hands.

"What does it do?"

"This instrument gathers any light available and intensifies it. It helps you see better in the dark."

After dinner, the trooper made the call to the police station before he came on the stoep. Annika kissed him on the cheek and had expected a reaction, but he barely noticed her gesture. They were talking when Angus came back, and McGovern stood mid-sentence.

"Come with me," he said and strode in the direction of the fence to the rear of the property. Once there he gave the scope to Angus. "Try it, push that button and you'll see a green light.

Angus did what he'd asked and although it wasn't a clear night, he could see into the dark clearly, only everything looked an eerie ghostly green color, kind of like a negative, but not.

"It will be better on a clear night," McGovern told him, "it's amazing on a moonlight night McGovern said of the new toy. Angus nodded his agreement because he could imagine that to be the case. On the way back to the stoep, McGovern told them he would be him on a week's leave saying they'd given that to him because he'd lost his partner.

Angus suggested a drink, went inside beer and came back with two beers and a bottle of brandy."

"You're a long way from home. You never told me how you came to be here," Angus probed.

"Long story." He began. "I grew up in Glasgow, left school without any qualifications had a string of crappie jobs, as long as it got me drinking money for the weekend. I started getting into trouble fighting, I was due for a court case and my lawyer told me I was facing jail time, so I went and signed up for the Paras for six years so they couldn't touch me.

"Drastic move," Angus claimed.

"Not at all, I loved training to be a paratrooper, loved the foreign travel, loved it right up to Ulster. The paramilitaries and others could shoot at us, but we couldn't shoot back, so as the government left us like sitting ducks, I packed it as soon as I'd done my six. They gave me the option of signing on again. Back on civvy street the only jobs I was offered were poxy security guard ones on pitiful money."

"So, you came here?"

He shrugged after brushing his hands down his thighs. "Not right away, I went to Angola. The job paid three times the money I'd been on with the Paras and I got to shoot back. It didn't take long to realise what a farce that was; they were told there were a few thousand mercenaries already there with more on the way. But when a group of one hundred and fifty arrived and it went tits up, I came to Rhodesia. At first, I thought here we go again, but the outfit didn't want Mercenaries, so I thought, what the hell and joined up."

Annika came to the stoep. "It's getting late," she said, dressed in a T-shirt and pants.

"I'll just bed down here on the stoep," McGovern said.

"No need, you can have my old room," she said, casually.

"Are you sure?" he asked, checking with Angus.

"Of course, it's not in use now anyway," Angus confirmed.

They all retired for the night and he changed into a pair of boxers and tee shirt while Annika went into the bathroom. She eyed his clothing and shook her head.

"Off," she commanded with a chuckle, gesturing toward him. "I am proud of you Angus McDonald," she said after they'd gotten into bed and they lay in the dark.

"For what?" he asked, puzzled.

"How confident you've grown." She kissed him, sighed, and fell asleep her head on his chest.

Angus woke early the next morning and slipped from the bed leaving Annika asleep. He knocked lightly on the bedroom door where McGovern slept. When he opened the door, the trooper stood dressed only in shorts, his light brown hair tussled.

"Shit, I could have slept all day," he informed Angus who told him to come to the kitchen for breakfast when he was ready.

Dova had prepared sliced meat, bread and fresh fruit and had already laid them on the table.

"I'm sorry for what Morton said the last time we were here. He was well out of order about you and Annika but, I'm glad you two are together now. Don't take this the wrong way, but Annika is gorgeous, you're a lucky man."

Angus was about to answer when the sound of the helicopter engine broke the early morning silence. McGovern grabbed his gear and as he reached the stoep the others began to emerge to see him off. They all shook hands and McGovern took off running the minute the machine touched down.

As was expected when it took off again leaves and other debris kicked up from the ground as it always did when choppers took off and he screwed up his eyes against the dust.

"You should have woken me up," Annika said as she came alongside him.

"You looked so peaceful," he said by way of explanation.

Weeks passed since McGovern's visit and the rains came less frequently. The dry season would soon be upon them. Dova and Anashe had started going out on alternate days with the patrols to gather the harvest nature had provided to help feed them, bringing back mango, figs, chillies, peppers and more, the list was endless. On the days they didn't go out with the patrol they spent laying out vegetables to dry on sheets raised on cut poles to keep the chickens and geese from eating them, making chutneys, and freezing others and storing root vegetables.

Most of the herd animals they'd had on the station had been released from the pens so they could make the trek north, following the rains.

Angus sat quietly reflecting in the shade of the Acacia tree; Manodno had made a bench next to the graves.

"Would you mind if I sit with you?" Annika asked in a quiet almost subdued voice as he stared into space.

"No... please sit," he told her pointing to the bench beside him.

As she sat down, he reached for her hand. She didn't know whether to speak or stay silent while Angus continued to stare into the sky.

"Do you think they know what's going on here?" he asked, softly.

Annika thought he was talking about the people buried next to where they sat. "I'm sure they will be watching over us"

Angus looked confused. "Who?"

She nodded at the graves and he smiled. "I didn't mean them, I meant the people in that plane," he said, pointing at an airplane high in the sky.

The little silver plane streaked northward, leaving four vapour trails behind that slowly merged in to one.

"I see them flying overhead... same time every day." Annika looked skyward with him. "Three miles straight up. That's all that separates us from this madness called Africa.

They sat in silence watching the plane until only the vapour trail was left.

"Why did you stay in Africa after..." she trailed off not knowing how to approach the subject of the massacre on the station.

Angus nodded in the direction of the graves. "I suppose at first I couldn't bear the thought of leaving Morag here on her own." He lapsed into silence for a bit and then sighed.

"And now?" she asked.

"Now Africa has is under my skin. Scotland is beautiful but in a much different way. Africa surpasses it, its paradise, if only the people would get along with one another. Every few kilometres it changes into another country."

"Tonight, I would like you to tell me all about Scotland," Annika prompts, changing the subject to break the solemn mood.

After dinner they were on the big cane couch on the stoop he was sitting, she lay down with her head on his thighs her glass of wine on the floor beside her Angus had a brandy resting on top of the earth filled flour sack at his elbow.

"Now tell me about Scotland I have seen pictures and films of it but never been there. What is it like?"

"For a small country people are very diverse. The lowlanders are less reserved and open than the highlanders... they're more suspicious of outsiders. There are many local dialects," I said when I thought of the Morton, McGovern and I in the way we spoke. Scottish people are all different but if you kick one of them, they all limp. It's a patriotic thing, historically they were very fierce warriors when they had to be, and had been the backbone of the British army for Centuries."

Annika raised a brow and he chuckled. "It's true. They wore highland dress with the kilt in battle the Germans in the First World War called them the women from hell.

She smiled. "And now I'm in love with a Scotsman in pants from heaven."

Angus went on to tell her how the lowlands and the highlands contrasted the green fields and forests of the lowlands the black granite mountains the mist and the rain and desolate moorlands of the north. "I would like to see it one day Angus. The Netherlands are so flat no mountains no hills will you take me?"

"Maybe someday you will, Annika," he replied in an uncertain tone.

CHAPTER 19

*A*ngus woke to the sound of retching coming from the bathroom before Annika came back into the bedroom wiping her flushed face with wet towel, her hair sticking to her to her face and shoulders with sweat.

"Are you alright," he asked as he jumped out of the bed. she nodded. "Must have been something you ate last night." Annika nodded again. "Do you want to stay in bed today?"

She flashed him a tired smile. "I've been sick, I am not ill, it's nothing to worry about."

Although she felt delicate Annika got on with her day. Since the rainy season had come to an end with only short showers of fine mist, the vegetation was starting to lose its colour and droop as the autumn African sun began its job of petrifying the red earth. With the beginning of May now upon them the work on the station would be minimal with only the animals indigenous to the area.

Most of the grazing animals had moved north following the rain, the dry season left them with time on their hands, time to do the jobs they could not do when the rains were here. Only short patrols were carried out there had been no military activity in the area for weeks, and only reports of insurgencies on the radio were in south around the area of the border with Botswana.

Dinner became a different affair only Angus, Annika, Lindani and Anashe ate on the stoep. The others ate in the kitchen.

"Annika you have to be careful what you eat, you've been sick quite a few times in the last three weeks," Angus told her in a concerned tone when she had taken a mouthful of Impala and rice.

Annika covered her mouth with her hand to stifle her smile. Anashe and Lindani grinned knowingly, got up and left the table.

"What did I say?" as he watched them vanish inside.

"You're so clueless sometimes. We're going to have a baby." He blinked once and stared for a long minute until she spoke again. "Sickness is one of the early symptoms in some women," she told him.

"Salisbury," he blurted. "We need to go to Salisbury."

"Why?"

"To get married… we need to get married."

Annika gave him a soft smile. "We don't have to get married; we're only having a baby together."

A look of disappointment crossed his face. "There's another reason I can't marry you."

"WHY! Why not?" he asked, his heart sank to his stomach.

"There's something you've forgotten."

"Forgotten?"

"You haven't asked me yet."

Angus wrapped his arms around her staring into her eyes. "Right," he said, nervously, "will you marry me?"

She nodded a beaming smile on her face. "Yes, I'll marry you, Angus."

Angus took off running from the stoep to the kitchen where everyone sat around the table wearing big wide grins. "She said yes, we're having baby. You'll be my best man, Lindani."

"Ask Angus, ask." Annika prompted from behind. She shook her head, smiling. They went back to the stoep the rest followed and sat around "Why have you all been eating separate from us?" Manodno.

"Lindani said Annika would tell you when the time was right so, we ate in the kitchen."

Angus stared at Lindani. "You knew?" he frowned, "How?"

"Anashe told me last week," Lindani replied.

They all broke in to fits of laughter and Manodno pointed to their untouched food.

"You have not eaten we will go and leave you to eat alone."

They left the stoep, some heading to the workshop, others to the kitchen and roof space.

As they ate Annika told Angus she hadn't wanted to tell him until she was sure.

"A ring, we haven't got a ring," he suddenly blurted dropping his fork full of food back onto his plate.

"There's plenty of time for all that, now eat your food, you have two people who need you now," she said through a chuckle. After they had ate, she confessed she was tired and went to bed.

Angus tided up before he crept into the bedroom in the dark, removed his shirt and slipped beneath the sheets beside her. Immediately Annika's hand wandered over trying to find his penis.

"Off," she said as she tugged at his shorts.

"We can't, were having a baby… you're having a baby."

She tugged again. "Off." This time he obeyed. Annika

rolled on top of him and straddled his waist. "Angus we don't have to stop making love because I'm pregnant."

"We might hurt it."

She laughed. "Angus the baby inside me is between the size of a grain of sand and a pinhead, you couldn't find it let alone hurt it."

"Still," he said, worriedly. Annika rose, took hold of his now hard length, and slipped it inside her.

"If you won't make love to me Angus McLean, then I will make love to you." Annika her hips, her need growing until she convulsed with pleasure. The sensation sent Angus over the edge as well. Afterwards she rolled onto the bed beside him. As their breaths settled, she said in the darkness. "I gave you a special present last Christmas, "meaning how she slept with him in the first place, "now if things go to plan, you'll have another special gift for the next one."

"Christmas presents?"

She sighed at how dense he was being. "The baby, Angus."

He paused. "January?"

She sighed again. "It's still April, Angus."

"Oh right, I see what you mean now," he said, chuckling.

Angus lay in the dark after Annika had fallen asleep and his thoughts of Morag. His eyes welled with tears as they had often talked about a baby. Eventually sleep overcame him and he drifted off to sleep.

The following morning, he woke to find Annika propped on one elbow staring down at his face after she'd kissed as his eyes opened.

"What's wrong?" he asked.

She kissed him again. "I was just thinking how fortunate I am to have found as gentle, and as loveable a man, as you." Angus smiled and put his arm across her waist as they lay facing one another. "Angus we don't have to do thing differently because I'm pregnant, if I feel uncomfortable about anything, I'll tell you, but you must also tell me." he nodded. "Now let's get the day started as it should," she said, pulling him on top of her as she rolled on to her back.

Later, she went to the surgery and began her end of season stock take, dressed in an orange shirt tied in a knot beneath her breasts and a pair of denim shorts. Angus was convinced they hadn't left a store frayed so high around her thighs. The contrast of colours highlighted her tanned legs and flat stomach and the green pendant he'd given her. He hadn't wanted to leave her alone so offered to help her stock take.

Every time an opportunity presented itself, he stroked her stomach. "Baby, my baby," he muttered in awe, unable to keep his hands off her. Annika couldn't stand it any longer.

"Angus would you please stop doing that?"

"but I'm only…" he paused "I'm sorry, but this is huge. I can't believe this is happening."

she shook her head. "I don't mind you touching me, but if you don't want me to make love to you right here in the surgery, you'll stop."

Manodno appeared at the door. "Angoos, Lindani says someone comes." He left and the door swung shut.

Annika stared wide eyed at him. "Now how would that have looked if I'd had my way with you?" Colour rose to his cheeks as he headed for the door shaking his head with a small smile on his lips.

Manodno was waiting outside the surgery pointing up to Lindani who was in the roof space.

"What can you see, Lindani" Angus shouted as they crossed to the stoep.

"Crocodile it's a Crocodile vehicle," he replied.

Mandala held the gate open as the heavy machine rumbled in and came to a halt at the foot of the stairs. The tailgates opened Ted Hibbins climbed down, waved, and made his way up the steps.

"Hello," I had some time on my hands I thought I'd take a trip here to see how you're doing, then carry on up to Matazari and check in with the guys up there."

He walked round introducing himself and shook everyone's hand before he, Angus and Annika settled on the stoep. The rest of the station members returned to what they'd been doing before his arrival. Dova brought a jug of iced tea and glasses to the table.

"How have you been getting on?" Ted asked.

"I'm pregnant no… no not me, Annika."

Ted raised his eyebrows. "Well, I will take it you're getting on okay," he laughed, "congratulations to you both." He shook Angus's hand Annika's with peck on her cheek. "Can I ask you something Angus?" he nodded. "Do you have a bloody beer instead of this cat's piss?"

Ted came from Yorkshire but had been in Rhodesia over twenty-five years, with the wildlife department for twenty. He'd been married twice but was divorced both times.

Angus went to the kitchen and came back with a bottle of beer and a glass, he put them in front of him Ted looked up "not joining me?"

Angus shook his head "We're having a baby."

Annika sighed. "Angus I am pregnant not you, now get a dam beer." He turned to go back but Dova had brought some to the table.

"Keep bringing them as long as they want," she told Dova. She glanced in Ted's direction, he winked and smiled. "I must get back to my stocktake. Are you staying tonight Ted?"

"If you don't mind," he said.

"Good, see you later then," she said and made her way down the stairs.

"By 'eck lad, you got yer hands full wi that one," he said through a chuckle.

"We're getting married as soon as we can get to Salisbury to arrange it," Angus informed him with a beaming smile.

"I could do the paperwork for you, but it might take a bit of time. Things don't always run as smooth as they used to."

Angus leaned closer. "Can you? Would you, Ted?"

Ted nodded. "We work for the administration; we have the authority to make special arrangements."

Angus pulled his head back but held his stare. "Do it, Ted."

"Don't you think you should ask you future wife first?"

Angus looked stunned. "Oh, I suppose."

Ted shook his head "What are you like lad? How did you get Morag here? Did you just tell her you had job in Rhodesia, or did you ask her if she wanted to come here?"

He shrugged. "A job's a job when you don't have one."

"No but did you ask her if she wanted to come?" Angus shook his head. "ell I think you going to find you're marrying a different kind of woman this time laddie."

After his talk with Ted Hibbins, Angus took his advice and as they got ready for dinner, he asked Annika how she felt about Ted planning for their wedding. Thankfully, Annika was all for it.

Before they sat down to dinner Angus asked Lindani to eat with the others to give Annika and himself some time alone with Ted to discuss the wedding. As they ate, they hashed out the details and decided they wanted a civil arrangement as soon as possible.

"Who will be your witnesses to the marriage?"

"Lindani and Anashe," Annika replied.

Ted nodded. Okay, now what I'm going to tell you I ask you not to repeat.

Annika interrupted him. "Ted can I ask you something?" He nodded. "Will you act as my father at our wedding? His face lit up with a smile. Angus was shocked because she had only just met him, but it seemed apt considering their strange situation.

"It would be my pleasure, thank you Annika," Ted replied, after his initial shock.

"Now listen to what I want to tell you. There are whispers circulating in Salisbury the government are talking about a deal with Zanu and Zapra— some sort of power sharing. I don't know how that will work out because both have the same Communist backers and the backers will want their share of the rewards."

"What does that mean?" Angus asked.

"Smith is under extreme international pressure from the Brits and the US.

Annika looked thoughtful. "So, we might end up with a Communist government?"

Ted pursed his lips and raised his eyebrows as he shrugged. "Remember these are just whispers not facts, but, if I were you, I'd make the most of your wedding. "Okay, the other thing I'm going to tell mustn't go any farther either." They both looked to each other and nodded. "First, do either of you have any savings?" Again, they both nodded. "Get as much as you can raise. I know a guy in Salisbury who can more than double it for you."

"Why?" Angus asked, confused why someone would do that.

"In case this political thing is true, and you have to get out."

They nodded their understanding of the whole picture if the government were to change.

"Come and see me before the wedding and I'll get you fixed up," Ted advised them.

"Ring, we need a ring, Ted," Angus blurted his thought at the mention of the wedding again.

Ted chuckled. "he's only got one thing on his mind."

Annika shouted Dova tell the others to join them if they wish and to bring more drinks. They all sat around the table.

"Only one beer for you Chatambuza and Mandala it's your turns for night watch, Mandala you have the scope?" They both nodded.

"You do a night watch?" Ted asked, surprised by this change in routine on the station.

Angus nodded "We've been doing it since we lost Dzingia." Landani nodded, confirming what Angus had said.

"You mentioned a scope?"

Angus asked Manodno to show it to Hibbins. "Starlight scope," he said giving it the full name McGovern had told him. "We took it from a Korean we killed that was part of the group who killed Dzingia."

Ted told him he heard about the night site instruments but had never actually seen one. Angus took him from the stoep to the side of the building where there was no light. The night was dark and moonless, but the sky was a blaze of stars horizon to horizon.

Angus gave him the scope. "Look though here and press this button."

Ted put the rubber pad to his eye. "Bloody hell lad. And these buggers are using shit like this against our lads? They don't have chance." Angus told him there were a couple of things the insurgents didn't have. "And what is that?

"Bush craft— the Rhodesian Light and the Selous scouts," he told him. The soldiers who had passed through the station had told Angus they were poorly trained. Twice he and the men at the station had caught and killed some of the insurgents.

"How many have you killed?"

Angus shrugged. "Dozens?"

When they arrived back at the steps to the stoep Angus

put his foot on the first step as Ted Hibbins clapped his huge hand on his shoulder.

"You need to be careful 'ere lad… and take care of that lass of yours." Angus nodded.

They sat alone on the stoep drinking brandy; Ted asked if he would show him the measures, they had taken to tighten security at Nyanga to see if he could pass any tips to Matazari or the other stations. He told him he would be glad to help.

Next morning while the driver of the Crocodile was making it ready, Ted asked Angus if he was ready to give him the tour. Angus took him to the roof space first showing him what they'd done with the roof and floor space. Ted stopped at the firing station looking over the front of the building pointing at the machine gun.

"It's an RPD Russian made weapon and we've got a second one over in the workshop. We got this one from the first kill we made. We've got another the RLI gave us over the workshop. This gives us at least two guns on any position around the station. Don't forget we have the cannons on the Croc for mobility as well. All the guys are good individual shots except for Banele, but he can still make one of these babies sing.

With the tour done, Ted shook hands with everyone as they said their goodbyes and when he shook Annika's hand, he kissed her on the cheek. He shook Angus's last and gave him a hug, whispering into his ear. "Remember, look after her lad," he said. With a final wave he climbed in the Crocs rear and it moved off.

CHAPTER 20

*O*ver the next few weeks everything dried out the vegetation was taking on is winter straw colour, little dust devils played in the breezes in the compound.

Angus had got the men on the station to burn back the dying vegetation when the wind was in the right direction, to maintain their field of fire. He had got agitated why had Ted hadn't been in touch about the wedding arrangements. Had he made it back to Salisbury? Every time he passed the office, he asked whoever was manning the radio if there was any word, always the same answer.

"I'm going to Nyanga tomorrow" he announced in the middle of the night to a sleeping Annika.

She sat up in the bed. "What? Why? What's brought this on?"

"I need to speak with Salisbury."

She frowned. "Why?"

"I need to find out what the holdup is with the wedding."

"It's the middle of the night, Angus," she said, tiredly.

"Okay, okay," he conceded and lay back on the bed.

In the morning, he was first to get up and had showered

and dressed before anyone else had woken up, anyone except Annika, because he'd made more noise trying to be quiet than he would have had he not tried. Lindani appeared on the stoep as he sat with Annika still in her tee shirt and pants.

"Ask Mandala to the get a Land Rover ready and tell him he's coming to Nyanga with me."

"Would it not be better if you took the Croc?" Lindani asked.

"No, that stays here. If there's any trouble, get them all inside that and go."

When they were ready to leave, he kissed Annika on the forehead as he set off. "Any trouble you stay beside Lindani." She nodded and as he turned to go, she rolled her eyes in her head toward Lindani and Anashe, they grinned.

They made it to Nyanga in record time, leaving dust clouds behind them; the speed they'd gone at was against all the training they had taught him, if a big animal such as a Kudu buck broke from cover from beside the narrow road or worse still, a Rhino. The Land Rover would not have offered enough protection from an impact of such a beast, and any collision would be devastating.

He braked in a cloud of dust outside the block-built building which was the police station and ran inside. It was one of the few structures in the village not made from timber.

"I need to use your phone," he demanded.

Corporal Nyasha sat on the other side of the desk. Angus had met him few times here at Nyanga and at the station. Nyasha was a slim young man from the Netebele tribe, whose people occupied an area where they and the Shona tribal lands over lapped. In years gone by it had been the area of fierce conflicts over the land, but the two tribes had co-existed in peace since the turn of the century.

"Do you have an emergency?"

Angus nodded as he lifted the handset from the receiver. As he began dialling, Nyasha got up from behind the desk, attaching his service revolver to the lanyard that hung from his shoulder.

"Farai, bring the Toyota out front and be ready to follow Angus."

Angus made his call and as he placed receiver back on the cradle ending the call, Nyasha scowled. "That didn't sound like an emergency call it was a social call please don't do that again."

"Six weeks… six weeks," he beamed.

"six weeks, what?"

Angus looked at the Corporal as though he was stupid "six weeks man, the wedding… my wedding, it's in six weeks." Angus turned to Mandala. "Right back to Nyanga station we have to tell them."

Mandala looked nervous. "Angoos, should we not have a cold drink and rest in the shade?"

Both their faces were caked red with dust. "I think we need to wash." Angus calmed his excitement and nodded in agreement.

They went to a corrugated shack that passed as a bar on the main street; he ordered two beers and asked if they had anywhere, they could wash. The barman directed him to a well pump behind the shack and they took it turns with the pump handle as they washed the off the earth.

Under the canvas shaded bar front they drank bottles of Rouge beer, another South African brew, while Mandala told Angus his driving had frightened him. He grinned but promised to drive slower on their return journey.

Back at the station, he broke the news to the others about the wedding; Annika told him it gave them plenty of time to prepare things.

As the following days grew into weeks Annika's once flat

stomach grew as well, gone were the shorts, now exchanged for loose fitting skirts, the tight vests replaced her looser items of clothing and some of Angus's. Angus was worse than ever, checking in that she still felt okay.

He spent the week before they were due to travel to Salisbury drawing up rotas for everyone who was staying behind in his attempt to make sure everything ran smoothly during their absence. Sunday night, the night before they left, he felt restless rising from the bed many times, and checking things over and over.

They set out in the Crocodile at first light the following morning. If Angus had got his way, they would have left the morning after the call came and waited in Salisbury. When they got on the main road, Annika kept telling him to slow down as it was not an iron road but compacted stone, making the ride extremely bumpy. Thankfully, they reached the outskirts of Salisbury just before noon in one piece.

"I have booked us all into the George?" she asked, confused.

"Booked us all in?"

He nodded. "Two rooms, I mean one for you and me, one for Lindani and Anashe."

He parked the crocodile in the hotel parking lot as he was finishing taking the Brownings from their mounts and securing inside the Crocodile a bell boy came and took their bags; only theirs — Lindani and Anashe carried their own.

Angus got a very different greeting at reception this time when he said they had rooms booked. The receptionist asked him to wait a moment. She went into a room behind the desk and came back with a short skinny guy with slicked down black hair, dressed in an evening suit.

He motioned Angus aside. "I'm the manager here and I'm afraid there's been some mistake with your booking, sir."

"The Department of Game booked the rooms," Angus told him.

"I understand that sir, but wouldn't your friends be more comfortable elsewhere?"

"I've always found the hotel very comfortable. I've stayed here every time I've come to Salisbury."

"I understand that, sir, but we have to think of our other guests." The manager's eyes shifted to Lindani who stood staring down at the floor.

Angus's face turn beet red with rage. He leaned into the short man's face and pointed to Lindani. "That man has killed for me and I for him. Now give him the fucking key before I shoot you."

All colour drained from his face to match starched shirt he was wearing, it was only then he noticed Angus was holding his R1.

Turning his pale face toward the receptionist the manager snapped, "Well don't just stand there you stupid girl, give our guests their keys."

"D… do you want help with you bags, sir?" he stuttered.

"Fuck off, we will carry them ourselves," Angus snapped again.

Nervous the manager edged toward the room behind him again. "Very well, as sir wishes," he muttered, and then he scooted back in where he came from.

The receptionist smiled, looking pleased at the outcome of the encounter. "Dinner starts at seven," she said, directing her comment toward Lindani.

"Can we lock these in the gun room?" he asked, gesturing toward the guns.

"I'll fetch the manager; he has the key." She went into the room at the back again but reappeared quickly with the key and a grin on her face. Her boss was obviously scared of Angus and didn't want to face him again. Lindani and Angus placed the guns in the rack and the receptionist locked the door.

They took the lift to their rooms Lindani and Anashe on the second floor, theirs on the top floor of the three-storey building. Angus dropped the bags in the suite he had chosen and looked at the view from the window.

"Angus come in here, quick," Annika shouted from the separate bedroom. When he couldn't see her, he went to the bathroom door, expecting some kind of crisis. She was pointing at the tub and he pushed her gently aside.

"What is it?" he asked, sounding alarmed.

"A jacuzzi, it's a jacuzzi."

"Jesus! Don't do that," he told her with his hand over his heart.

"Do what?"

"I thought there was a snake or something in there."

"I can handle animals, Angus, I'm a vet, remember?"

"Yeah, you can, but I'm not always sure that I can handle you."

When Annika advanced toward him, he saw the glint in her eye and knew they'd be in bed in minutes if she had her way.

"Oh, no you don't. We're going to the bank," he told her sternly, slapping her on her bottom.

"Oh! You're a spoilsport."

"Get changed we have a lot to do," he told her with a smirk on his face.

Annika asked Lindani and Anashe if they had wanted to join them when they went out, but he politely declined.

"It's Anashe's first time in Salisbury and I want to show her around," he explained.

Leaving the hotel, the couple went first to Annika's bank and requested a statement from her account at the ING bank in Amsterdam. Yannie's insurance and pension had been going in since his death along with other policies; she had never had to use the money as she had earnings of her own. She was told she had to go back the following day for this.

Next, Angus went to the First Rand bank and got a statement from his South African account; seventy-two thousand US dollars, a large amount in Rand or seventy-five thousand in Sterling. In his Rhodesian Reserve bank account, there was seventeen thousand US dollars. That gave him eighty-nine thousand. In Annika's Rhodesian account, she had twenty-one thousand. They withdrew the money in the Rhodesian accounts.

When they got back from the round at the bank, the receptionist told Angus he had a message. She passed him a piece of paper and he saw it was from Ted Hibbins asking him to call. He tried to return his call immediately, but he had gone home for the day.

They went to the bar lounge and ordered an orange juice for Annika and a beer for himself. As he took the first sip, he noticed two guys at another table dressed in shorts and shirts who looked familiar. He knew who the first man was, but it was a few seconds before he recalled the second man's name.

They were McGovern and Van-Rooyen. Each time he saw them they looked bedraggled and dirty. They got up from their seats and came over but didn't sit down.

"I have had a complaint about you," Van-Rooyen said, standing over him. Angus's eyes darted over toward the bar and he noticed the manager he'd spoken to before smiling behind the bar. "I heard you're threatening to shoot people."

"He was embarrassing my friend, what would you have done if it was Fudzai?"

Van-Rooyen shrugged, "I wouldn't have threatened to shoot him," he replied.

"Well, what would you have done?" Angus asked McGovern.

"I'd have shot him, not threatened to do it. The bastard would already be dead."

As they broke into laughter, he noticed Lindani had appeared, ready to have his back. His hand dropping from behind his back to his side and his shirt hem fell back to his waist. Angus instinctively knew Lindani had taken hold of the skinning knife he wore on his back, and he'd had been ready to protect them if the situation had warranted it.

He nodded past them to Lindani. "Do you want to say hello?"

Both men looked shocked they hadn't heard him arrive.

"Where the hell did you come from? It's good to see you, Lindani," McGovern stated.

"It is always better to see me," Lindani replied, grinning.

McGovern shouted over to the manager behind the bar. "Harry beers all round and orange juice for the ladies," he ordered.

He sent a server with the drinks McGovern gestured with his head toward the manager. "That's Dempie's brother-in-law — he can't stand the prick."

Once they had caught up and had a few more beers, Van-Rooyen and McGovern left. Both couples changed and had dinner, but as Angus felt tired after the drive, they headed upstairs to bed. Annika showered then filled the jacuzzi but when she went back into the bedroom Angus was sound asleep on top of the bed in his boxers. Not wishing to disturb him, she returned to the bathroom. She turned the jacuzzi off and drained it before she joined him on the bed, snuggling up to his back.

The following morning, he called Ted just after eight. Ted asked if they could come and see him at ten o'clock. They agreed they left Lindani and Anashe to carry on exploring Salisbury.

The taxi dropped them at the department building. Ted

shook hands with them and warned them he had little time, as he had a meeting with the finance minister and other department heads all day.

Ted then told them he had booked their wedding for three o'clock on Thursday afternoon at the registrar's offices. He informed them they had to be there by two fifteen with their passports to complete the paperwork and informed Angus he'd need to collect copy of his wife's death notification at the same office beforehand.

Ted then asked if they had sorted their finances out and they told him they had the money ready. He handed Angus a slip of paper. "See this guy he'll sort you out." He then he apologised for the rush, but his car was coming round to collect him but paused and told them he would buy them dinner tonight to meet in their hotel lobby at eight they shook hands and left.

"He's adopted you." Angus said as stepped back into the sunshine holding hands.

"What do you mean?"

"He never kisses me on the cheek," Angus said through a chuckle as he hailed a taxi.

He told the driver the address on the slip of paper, and ten minutes later they arrived at their destination. Angus paid the driver while Annika climbed out, and when he had driven off, they turned and entered the shop.

The place was brightly lit with display cases full of assorted jewellery and watches.

"What can I do for yer mate?" asked a voice with a West End London accent.

"Ted Hibbins sent us to see John Green?" the guy saluted his acknowledgement and told his assistant to watch the shop.

John gestured towards the rear of the shop for them to

follow and took them into a small office. He he closed the door, quietly.

"What can I do for you?"

Angus told him Ted said he could sort out the wedding gifts.

"Depends, what you want," he replied.

Angus shrugged his shoulders because he hadn't thought about it at all.

"When do you need them for?"

"Thursday," Angus said.

"Can you come back later this afternoon about five?" John asked. Both Annika and Angus agreed.

As they left, Angus checked his wristwatch. It was just before noon. "Five hours to kill," he informed Annika. The heat of the city with the sun being deflected from the buildings they were getting hot and sweaty.

"Let's get a taxi back to the hotel and if Anashe is back, I'll take her shopping," Annika said.

"And what am I supposed to do, take Lindani shopping?" Annika laughed at the way Angus pouted at her. By the time they got out of the taxi the heat was unbearable, their now damp cold clothes stuck to their skins.

Angus paid the driver, and they took the hotel elevator to the third floor and back to their suite. The room was cool, thanks to the air conditioning. Annika, she went straight to the bathroom and turned on the shower. The phone rang and Angus answered.

"Mr Angus McDonald?"

"Yes, who is this?"

"It's the registrar's office. I'm just confirming your booking to marry Mrs Annika Vandekamp nee Mulder at three o'clock on Thursday of this week. Is this information correct?"

"Yes."

"Thank you, as we arranged it in your absence, we have to check the details." The woman reminded Angus of the documentation both he and Annika had to present and concluded the call.

Annika walked into the lounge, towelling her hair.

"Who was that?" Angus informed her before heading into the bathroom. The steam from the shower had condensed and ran down the wall tiles. He ran the cold water in the shower and his skin drew tight in response. After a few minutes he his body became used to it and the shower had cooled him down.

When he finished his shower, he found Annika lying across the bed naked, her eyes closed, and her feet touching the floor. The air from the cooling unit above the bed helping her relax. He crossed the room and stood above her, but she didn't move, her breathing slow and rhythmic as she slept. Angus sat down on one of the two small armchairs and watched her sleep.

His thoughts turned to when they first met, the way he'd thought she was tormenting him, the way she thought he was ignoring her and marvelled at how their relationship had changed. Annika, she gave a little moan and her legs twitched. He rose from the chair and crossed over to her. He touched her knee lightly, and they parted.

He knelt and began kissing her knee, her legs parted in response. He ran his tongue gently along her thigh and when he reached the apex of it; she took his head in her hands and lead his face to her vagina. Her body twitched when his tongue probed her wetness. He slipped one finger then another into her as he sucked and kissed her clitoris. Annika shuddered with pleasure as her wetness mingled with his saliva on his chin.

"I could eat you, Annika," he whispered, softly.

She pulled his face up to hers and he lay over her. He had

needed encouragement as he slipped inside her and they stayed locked together as one. He took her until she shuddered in ecstasy and he pulsed inside her. When they had recovered from their intimacy, he looked at the table side clock; it was four fifteen.

"Shit, look at the time." They both showered together again to save tie and quickly dried themselves with the still damp towels. They slipped in two shorts and shirts while Angus called reception and ordered a taxi.

CHAPTER 21

The taxi dropped them outside the jewellers, the sign on the door said closed Angus tried the door, it was locked. Then he saw the man they had met earlier. He unlocked the door and let them in. The shop's interior was dimly lit now with a small desk lamp on the counter, he went behind the counter and offer his hand Angus took it in his when he tried to let go, he kept his grip "sorry what did you say your name was?" he looked surprised, "Oh right my name is Green... John Green" he loosed his grip, "pleased to meet you I'm Angus."

The man held his hand up "I know who you are" as he reached for Annika's hand. "Shall we get down to business?" Angus nodded.

"How much can you afford?" the man asked what he meant.

"Ted has told me to do you an escape package?" Angus looked confused. "A what! We're getting married Thursday, not escaping from anywhere."

He held his hand up, stopping Angus from going any further. "It's a package to be used if in the future if you

149

decide to leave Rhodesia in a hurry." Angus opened his mouth with an 'ah' look, like the penny finally dropped.

"OK how much money can you lay your hands on?" Angus looked at Annika. "Thirty-five thousand?" He disclosed and looked at Annika as if to confirm this with her. She nodded.

"OK I can do you a package that will at least treble that if you sell on the western market. With the sanctions we can only do diamonds or any other precious minerals domestically." Bending, he took a ring from a display beneath the counter and held between his fingers. This sells for one thousand four hundred pounds here, in London… you'd pay about six to eight thousand pounds sterling.

"That's insane," Angus mused.

His eyes narrowed in on Annika. "You've been married before?"

"I have."

"Here in Rhodesia?"

She shook her head. "Utrecht, in the Netherlands."

He looked relieved and nodded. "Okay, I can do this deal. Bring the money and your passport tomorrow morning," the jeweller tells them. "I will call you a taxi to take you back to your hotel."

When the taxi arrived, the broker let them out. Angus stared up at the shop as he settled in his seat. As he was it looking the light went out and the shopfront was plunged into darkness.

They travelled in silence on the way back to the hotel, both trying to absorb what had taken place at the jewellers. Once they were in the privacy of their room, they discussed their concerns about the meeting and found it neither could make their mind up whether they should go through with the deal he proposed or not. They headed down to the lounge bar and ordered soft drinks for them both. As the server placed them on the table, Ted's voice came from behind. "I'll have beer, please." The server signalled he'd heard him and left us as Hibbard sagged into a spare chair by Annika. "What a bloody day I've had."

"That bad huh?" Angus teased and Hibbard looked glared back at him. Fortunately for Angus, the server came back, breaking the tension between them. Instead of a comeback Ted just grunted, picked up the bottle and down his beer down his throat. He immediately signalled for a refill.

As the second beer went past his lips, Ted turned more mellow. "How did you get on with Green?"

"He knows we have thirty-five grand, and he wants to do a deal tomorrow. Question is, can we trust him Ted?"

Ted narrowed his eyes as he looked first at him, then towards Annika. "Thirty-five, eh? That would be around a hundred grand sterling," he paused, "if I think what happened with my sister's investment, she put up twenty and got sixty back home. She wishes she'd put more up, he's sound."

You can trust him, he's sound. He ordered another beer, drawing his hands down his face before confessing, "I wasn't sure what to do."

Angus frowned, confused by what he meant. "Do about what?" He sighed and Angus knew immediately whatever Ted was about to share wasn't good news. "I'm not sure whether to tell you before or after your wedding. Today the department had its budget cut by a third. We need to close stations… Nyanga might be one of them."

"What about the staff?" Angus asked, instantly depressed by the news.

"The final details haven't been worked out yet. We only got the news at two o'clock.

The server cut into the tense conversation. "Are you

151

dinning tonight?" Angus waved him away, too upset to eat right then, but told him to bring more beers.

"Not for me, I'm not good company tonight," Hibbard said and stood up to leave. Annika stood up put her arm around his neck and kissed him on the cheek. His eyes welled with tears and they both could see how the decision he'd learned about had affected him.

After Hibbard had gone Annika and Angus sat in silence, trying to absorb what it could mean, until Lindani and Anashe came into the lounge. "Aren't you having dinner?"

"I ate earlier, but you go ahead," nudging Annika to join them. She took his cue, stood to go with them and touched his shoulder as she left.

All three returned to the lounge after dinner, but Angus wasn't there, so Annika said goodnight to Anashe and Lindani and headed upstairs to bed. When she reached the suite, she went to the bedroom she found Angus face down diagonally on the bed, with his head on his forearm, still dressed but fast asleep. Deciding not to disturb him, she crept back into the lounge, switched off the light as she went and closed the bedroom door. Once in the lounge part of the suite she lay on the sofa thinking it had been a busy day, and in minutes she drifted off, exhausted.

Annika woke with a start the next morning with Angus standing in the bedroom doorway. "What do you think you're doing?"

"You were asleep when I came up to bed. I didn't want to disturb you," she told him. "Annika, you're pregnant, darling. You need the rest more than me."

She shook her head and gave him a wry smile. "Angus, I know what the station means to you, the way you care for everyone there. Yesterday's news from Hibbard has been a tremendous blow to you."

He sighed. "Let's get that ring on your finger then I will

worry about what comes next." She gave a dry sarcastic cough, and he corrected himself. "We can worry about it."

She grinned. "That's more like it. Let's get a quick shower, dressed and get to the bank… and I mean we're just having a shower."

Before they left to hotel room, Annika gathered up their dirty clothes and put them in a laundry bag which she left it outside the door.

At the bank they each had a fifteen thousand bankers draught drawn up and Annika drew five thousand I cash. She also enquired about her request she had previously made for her account enquiry at ING. The teller went to investigate, and when she returned; she handed Annika a sealed envelope. She thanked the teller for her help before she left.

Once outside, she opened the envelope, and her eyes went wide.

"What is it?" Angus asked when she remained silent.

"When she still didn't reply, she handed the slip of paper to him.

Angus stared at it, then stared at her. It was in Dutch Guilders.

"It's in Dutch," he says, frowning. "How much is that?"

"I think almost two hundred and fifty thousand pounds sterling." They hugged each other there in the street, stunned silent by their unexpected good fortune. "I don't care if you don't marry me now," she joked. Angus broke the hug and looked crestfallen for a second until she elbowed him in the ribs. "I'll just buy you instead," she smiled and kissed him.

They hopped in a taxi which dropped them at Greens shop. The trepidation of parting with thirty-five thousand now seemed irrelative, since they thought their future financial future looked more secure. They handed him the bank drafts over after he took them into his office in the back. He asked Annika the date she got married to her late husband

and wrote it down, his name and address at the time of their marriage.

When she asked why, "later," was all he said. "And your passport," he continued with his hand open to receive it. Annika handed it over to him. He flicked through the pages and handed it back to her.

"What are you going to do with all of this? Angus asked.

"I'll explain later," he replied. Before Angus could ask anything else, the jeweller and budding money broker went to a big safe opening the door he took out a flat black box and handed it to Annika. She cracked the box open by undoing the little hook and unhinging it. Lying on a bed of blue silk lay a heart-shaped clasp on a chain in the clasp was a huge sparkling diamond with two smaller diamonds either side of it. They were a matching pair of earrings, she gasped. "These are beautiful."

The jeweller in him smiled at her appreciation of the pieces. "These are not to wear, they're insurance." Angus stood and reached for the box, but the jeweller put his hand over it. "Come back at four o'clock and you can pick it up. I'll see you out." They were back on the street before they could comprehend what had just happened.

"Ted said to trust him," Angus said, but he sounded as if he was reassuring himself more than Annika. When they got a taxi back to the hotel, Lindani and Anashe were sitting in the garden in the shade.

"Come on, Anashe" Annika said to her, "girls shopping time." Anashe climbed into the taxi and when it had gone, Angus ordered two beers. As both men sat in the shade, Angus asked Lindani if he would track him later in the afternoon. Without asking Angus the reason for this, he nodded and then Angus told him about the threat to the authorities closing the station.

"I'll find out more tomorrow maybe," he told him.

"Tomorrow you get married, do not worry about the station," Lindani replied.

Later, the women returned from their shopping trip in time for Angus and Lindani joined Annika in the taxi, leaving Anashe behind. They headed for Green's shop again at three forty in the afternoon. Fifty yards before the jeweller's store, Angus asked the driver to stop. As he did, Lindani slipped out the door. When the couple entered the shop, there was another couple looking at rings; Green motioned for Angus and Annika to follow him to the office.

He handed Annika a receipt; it was from a jeweller's store in Amsterdam, dated a week before her marriage to Yannie. It had been written in Dutch, it had been made out to Yannie and had his home address. All that was written in the description column was diamond wedding gift set and the price of ninety-one thousand Guilder paid in cash.

Annika read it to Angus "What is this for?" he asked.

"Well, if you leave the country, this is proof Mrs Vandekamp brought it into the country with her. He handed over the box… but it was not the same box, it was an older one. Angus opened it to check the contents. "We couldn't allow you to have a new box with a receipt for the contents that are nine years old. Now," he said, "let me give you both something. He handed Angus a small square box. Angus opened them and inside were two gold wedding bands.

"These should fit," he told them. "I'll show you out." The jeweller slipped the two boxes in a bag.

Back in the hotel Angus went to the reception and asked if he could put a package in the safe pale faced Harry was happy to oblige and after he safely deposited the valuables, the two couples went to have dinner.

"Are you ready for your last sleep as a free man, Mr Mclean," Annika teased.

Angus looked at her with a serious expression on his face. "I won't be sleeping with you tonight."

Her jaw dropped, and her eyes widened. "Why the hell not?"

"It's bad luck to see the bride on the day of the wedding."

She laughed "Don't be silly."

"No, I'm having none of it. I'm sleeping in Lindani's room and Anashe is sleeping with yours in our room.

Once Annika knew he wouldn't budge on the matter, she stopped protesting.

NEXT MORNING, Angus ordered and ate breakfast on the small balcony in Lindani's room. Lindani collected his suit for the wedding, and he gave him the box with the two rings. The taxis were ordered to arrive ten minutes apart his at two p.m. and Annika's at ten past the hour.

When he arrived at the registrar's office at ten past two, Lindani sat waiting while Angus filled in his paperwork. Annika arrived just as they came out of the side office afterwards. She looked stunning in the loose orange dress, her blonde hair highlighting her golden tan, and when her emerald eyes met Angus's his heart melted at the sight of her. He never really heard the sermon to mesmerised by the beautiful woman he was making his wife.

Lindani glanced over his shoulder and gave him and nudge, which made the words of the registrar sink in, "You may kiss you bride." He kissed Annika with his eyes closed and was startled when muffled hands started clapping. Breaking their kiss, he turned and saw four Light Infantry Troopers dressed in their number one black uniform, with complete with their black berets and with white belts. Ewan, Kiwi, Jacko, and Bass stood proud and next to them the three

Selous Scouts, looking their best dressed in their unfamiliar green uniforms with red berets, green shirts with the gold winged Osprey emblems. Van-Rooyen Fudzai and McGovern all grinned in unison. Angus didn't even know if the scouts had a uniform, he'd never seen it before. They all wore white gloves to mark Angus and Annika's special occasion. Ted said to Angus, "You've made some delightful friends in some very ugly professions." Angus glanced toward the men and nodded. He agreed they were great friends, doing dirty work.

Everyone moved on to restaurant Ted had booked for the wedding dinner, an Italian restaurant. The staff were immediately wary and didn't know what to expect from the clientele, as some troops they had in the past had become a bit boisterous.

"As you're here for a week, come and see me in a few days when you're ready, bring Lindani as well, then we can begin to sort a few things out," Ted told Angus as they ate. Angus didn't want to think about work, it was his wedding day.

The evening passed without incident and Angus made a short speech, thanking everyone for coming and thanked Annika his new wife for taking a chance on him. All the men cheered with one calling out, "Lucky Bastard." Angus held his drink up and saluted them in agreement.

Ewan told him the drinks were on the RLI they owed him a pub.

"We'll drink to that," Van-Rooyan replied.

Fudzai presented the happy couple with cloth Selous patches, before turning to Lindani address Lindani.

"Why don't you come and get a proper one?"

The banter flowed back and forth between the two regiments for the rest of the evening, and Ted was steaming drunk by the time he ordered a taxi. Staggering, he shook everyone's hand as he left and kissed Annika on both cheeks.

"You're going to leave me for him aren't you," Angus joked. Annika, she punched his arm bicep gently and smiled.

"Give us a shout if she gets abusive with you, Angus," Ewan said and laughed.

"Can we go home," Annika whispered to Angus short time later. He grinned and winked at her.

"Okay, guys, we've had a long day…" Angus began.

"Yeah, yeah," came the taunts.

"And you want a longer night," McGovern replied.

"All right, all right," he said, smirking sheepishly. "I have to admit I would rather spend the night with my beautiful wife than sit here drinking with you hairy lot." A cheer went up as he waved the server and asked him to get them a taxi.

"For everyone?" the server asked.

"Okay, four taxis," he told the relieved server. When they got to their room, a bunch of twelve orange Konfetti roses and a bottle of twenty-five-year-old Talisker single malt whiskey sat on the dressing table. The card in the envelope read, "We hope the gold and the orange have many years together." Angus looked puzzled until Annika explained.

"The orange is for the House of Orange, the royalty of the Netherlands."

"The gold liquid is the water of life," he said.

She smiled, "Well, in that case, Angus McLean, you had better stop drinking brandy and beer, and start drinking that, because I'm going to need you for a long, long time."

CHAPTER 22

*A*fter a long night of lovemaking, they woke the next morning and had breakfast together with Lindani and Anashe in the dining room. As they were finishing pale face Harry approached their table carrying a tray with a jug of orange and a bottle of champagne.

He mixed the drinks in the five fluted glasses on the tray then held his up.

"To the bride and groom." They all toasted, he told them the drinks were on behalf of the management.

Harry then asked Lindani if he could have a word with him, Angus was going to interject, but Lindani got up and walked off with him. Angus began to worry but Lindani came back a few minutes later smiling.

"What did he want?" Angus asked.

"He was apologising for when we arrived."

"Not before fucking time," he said.

Annika, she shook her head.

"Angus!" he looked at her sheepishly.

"Sorry for cussing."

As they finished the buck's fizz, he asked what the plans

for the day were. Lindani told him Anashe wanted to see more of Salisbury. The couple agreed to meet later and went off to get ready to sightsee.

When they had gone Annika said she felt tired with the travel and all the rushing around. She suggested they laze by the pool. Fifteen minutes later they stretched out on sun loungers under a thatched roof gazebo.

For the rest of the morning, they dozed on and off, then had a light lunch of salad at a poolside table, before spending the rest of the afternoon in the shade under the gazebo. Lindani and Anashe came back from their day out and joined them for the last hour. Gradually, they all made their way to their rooms to shower and change for dinner, agreeing to meet up in the bar at eight.

The air-conditioning had been left running all day with the widows closed and felt freezing after their day in the blistering sun. Angus turned it off and opened the windows, and once again, the heat of the day came flooding in.

"Will you do something special for me?" Annika asked.

He took her in his arms. "Anything you want, love."

Gently Annika pushed him away by his chest and looked into his eyes. "Would you get the box from the safe? I would like to try the diamonds on."

He left the room and went to the reception to for the safe to be opened. Pale face Harry asked him to follow him back. He opened the safe and Angus retrieved the box.

Back in the room he heard the buzz of the Jacuzzi motor whirr as he closed the suite door, and went into the bedroom, placing the box on a bedside table before he joined her in the bathroom.

Annika was sitting with her head back and eyes closed as the water bubbled furiously around her. As soon as she heard him, she opened her eyes and sat forward, looking excited.

"Did you get them?"

"Yup."

"Can I try the jewels on?" Without replying, Angus went back to the bedroom and brought back the box.

"They're yours. Wear them whenever you like."

Annika moved nearer while in the tub and knelt in front of her husband. "Will you put the necklace on?"

Angus opened the box and took it out. It was the first time he had really studied it and gasped when he realised there was a diamond the size of his thumbnail. Three smaller diamonds were set in the gold chain at equal distances on either side, decreasing in size. Even the smallest was at least a full carat. She turned her back to him, lifting her wet hair, as he tried to unclasp the Emerald chain she wore.

"Leave it on" she said and pushed the emerald over her shoulder with her free hand, so it lay down her back.

Angus lowered the diamond necklace over her head and fastened the delicate clasp. As he removed his hand, his wife stood up and turned to stand directly before him.

"How do I look?" Beads of water streamed down her glistening body as the diamonds sparkled against her tanned skin.

"No diamond could make you look any better than you already do without them." she sat down again. "Damn, get in here, my gorgeous husband."

Angus removed his clothes and lowered himself into the pleasantly warm water, stretching out his legs. Annika opened her legs to let him put his feet between them.

"Have you gone off me now that we are married?" she teased.

He looked at her, stunned. "What do you mean?"

She smiled. "We've been married for over twenty-four hours and you have not made love to me on one occasion." She slid down so his toes now pressed on her bush; his body reacted immediately as his erection grew as the bubbles from the pump stimulated his balls. Annika knelt and came over to his side of the Jacuzzi and settled between his legs, placing her back against his chest.

Angus stroked down her arms gently, slid his wet fingers around to her nipples and tweaked them. He bent and kissed the back and side of her neck. Her nipples stood proud and hard while he gently rolled them between his fingers. Shifting, she lifted herself and sat on his thighs, reached underneath her, and fisted his penis. She positioned herself above him and took him inside. She started gyrating slowly, and he dropped one hand from her nipple, rubbed her stomach gently, then worked it down to her clit.

When he found her tender spot, he began circling it. As he rubbed it grew harder and Annika ground down harder against him. As she got faster, she reached down and touched his hand "faster harder faster," she chanted before she went over the edge with a scream. "Shit, oh God." He came inside her with a groan, his seed emptying inside her.

They sat fighting to regain their breath for a long time until he had shrunk still inside her. "Wow" she said as she slid off him and stood up. His seed dripped from her and ran down her thighs as he lay there, unable to move or not wanting to. He got out and switched the Jacuzzi off and opened the drain. When he went into the bedroom, his wife was lying on her back across the bed, her legs spread, his juice clung to the blonde hair around her opening. He went back into the bathroom and ran the taps on the Jacuzzi with warm water and added bath lotion. As it filled, he went back to the bedroom.

"What are you doing?" she asked.

"Running a bath for us."

"Why? We've just been in the jacuzzi."

"If we don't bathe, the smell of sex will be stronger that the smell of food in the restaurant." she started laughing, but saw it obviously unsettled Angus, so she agreed. As they bathed, they washed each other.

The phone started ringing in the bedroom. Angus got out of the bath and went to answer it, leaving a trail of water dripping from his body.

It was Lindani asking if they had changed their minds about dinner; he asked the time Lindani told him it was ten minutes after eight. Annika hadn't felt too well he lied but told him she was ok now and they were getting ready. They took the box of jewels back and had them locked in the safe, then went to the restaurant.

Over dinner Annika asked Anashe if she would go shopping with next day, she had to buy maternity wear as her clothes were becoming too tight around her waist.

* * *

AT MIDDAY FOLLOWING MORNING, the two women set off on their shopping trip. Angus had called Ted and arranged a meeting with him and Lindani for two o'clock. The two men decided to walk the few kilometres to the department offices on the other side of town. As they walked, Angus told Lindani he didn't know what was going to happen. All he knew was Nyanga was on a list of stations to be closed. What was going to happen to the staff was still to be decided?

4Ted came to the reception area a few minutes after the receptionist had told him they had arrived. After shaking hands, he took them to find somewhere they could meet and get a cold drink.

They sat in the shade of a huge, coloured parasol advertising Becks Pilsner beer. Angus asked the server for one and laughed when he told him they only had Sibebe. he had never heard of it, he told him it came from Swaziland.

They ordered three and a plate of beef sandwiches. As

they ate them Ted confirmed three stations were to be closed over the next six months. He asked Lindani he could come to Salisbury with Anashe where he could attend a business management course and told him they would be allocated a house, the course would be still be paid by the department, in the event if Nyanga was picked. Lindani told him he would ask Anashe.

Hibbard and Angus arranged a meeting with Annika over dinner, and Angus agreed to book a restaurant and let him know where. He offered to give them a ride back to the hotel, but Angus told him they would walk back to the hotel as the heat of the day was cooling.

The two men walked back in silence. Hibbard told them at dinner Nyanga was on the list for closure. Angus asked Lindani what his first thoughts were on Teds offer. He told him he didn't know. He had lived in the Nyanga valley all his life and he was a bushman not a city dweller.

Angus told him not to make any quick decisions as there could be a future, with a business management degree, and it did not have to be with the department. He could go elsewhere. At the hotel they sat with Annika and Anashe and went over what Ted had told them, they asked questions they could not answer all they could tell them stations were to be closed.

He and Annika sat in the foyer just before eight she wore a sky-blue maternity dress she had bought that day. Angus thought she looked pretty.

He disclosed how disappointed he was that after everything that had happened and all the work, he'd put in it felt it was all for nothing, since Nyanga was likely to close, and all his friends were to be split up.

"I dread telling them."

Ted came into the foyer asking if they were ready. They got into his taxi and the ride to the restaurant took ten minutes. They travelled most of it in silence. Angus asked if Ted liked Asian food, he said he did.

The restaurant was dimly lit with Asian music played in the background mingled with the smell of spices; a waiter showed them to a booth and lit a candle as they were taking their seats. They ordered drinks and picked their choices from the menus. As they ate,

Ted asked Annika if she would consider what he was about to propose in the if or when Nyanga closed. He said he could offer her the post of head of veterinary at the department based in Salisbury, and Angus, deputy head of department, his assistant. The rest of the dinner was spent in friendly chat with no more mention of Nyanga.

"Annika, how are you feeling now?" She looked puzzled. "Lindani told me you weren't feeling that well last night."

Annika looked at her husband who had spun the lie to Lindani.

"It was just a headache, but she's been fine today," Angus said, saving his wife's blushes. Angus told Hibbard they intended to leave the day after tomorrow.

* * *

WHEN THE TAXI pulled away from the hotel entrance, they waved Hibbard off and went inside, Lindani and Anashe were sitting at a table by the window in the bar, they went and joined them. They ordered drinks and told the couple about the talk they had with Ted over dinner and what he had proposed to them.

"That would mean we would be together here in Salisbury?" Anashe asked.

Annika told her they told her it wasn't that easy as they would have to discuss his offer and what it would mean to their lives.

As Angus downed the last of his whiskey, he held the glass up motioning to the server. When he came to the table, he ordered two doubles, a glass of water, a white wine for Anashe, and another orange juice for Annika. When the drinks arrived, he placed one double and the glass of water in front of Lindani. He picked the glass up and put the rim to his nose.

"It smells like the surgery," he said they all laughed at his description.

"Slange a var," Angus said and took a mouthful, rolling it around his mouth. Lindani did the same as his eyes started to water, and he swallowed. He grabbed the glass of water and took two gulps with tears now running down his cheeks.

"It burns," he said.

"It is the water of life," Angus told him.

"It is more like the kiss of death," his friend replied. "How do people drink this?" Angus told him it was the national drink in Scotland.

As Angus ordered another, he asked Lindani "same again?" He shook his head he had not ventured a second sip on the first one and stuck to his beer instead. When they finished their drinks, they made their way to their rooms. As he closed the door and made his way to the bedroom, he was staggering the wine with dinner and the whiskies had taken their toll.

When sat on the bed, Annika had to undress him. He rolled onto the bed in his boxer shorts. Annika left him and went to get ready for bed. When she returned, he was snoring.

Next morning, he woke and sat on the edge of the bed with a hangover while Annika slept beside him. He sat with his head in hands, his temple drumming inside it. His mouth felt like something had died in there.

He crossed to the bathroom and ran the shower, having

set the temperature on warm. He stood with closed eyes the force of the spray landing on the back of his neck and shoulders. He opened his eyes and looked down. He still had his boxers on. He had to hold on to the mixer valve to remove them or he thought he would fall over. Edging the temperature controller towards the cold symbol until it ran cold and stood there until he started to shiver. Once dried and five minutes with the toothbrush and mouthwash he felt better, only the drummer in his head to take care of now, two aspirin and thirty minutes later he was ready to face the day. He sat on one armchair in the lounge until Annika came from the bedroom still wearing her tee shirt and pants; she smiled.

"Have you been up long?"

"Too long," was the answer. She showered, dressed, and they went for breakfast. Lindani and Anashe had already finished eating and were having a cup of tea. Annika ordered a full breakfast, while Angus had tea and toast.

"We need to start getting things ready to go back to Nyanga tomorrow." He and Lindani ran around gathering everything they wanted to take back to the station and went to stow them in the Crocodile that was parked at the back of the hotel. The heat inside was like a furnace and the heat hit him in the face and the smell of gun oil was nauseating. It had sat in the sun for over a week with the roof turret closed.

When the heat had dissipated from the interior of the Crocodile before they unloaded their eight crates of different brands of beers and three cases of brands into the back. When they were locked up the Crocodile, they joined the women by the poolside and are outside on their last evening. As the sun threw its last beams down on them and their shadows lengthened by the time, they went to their rooms to get ready for dinner.

Annika went straight to the bathroom and opened the

taps on the Jacuzzi, telling him it might be long time before they would get the chance to have another one. He turned the pump on and poured a little bubble bath liquid in just enough to make it foam on the surface.

She was first to get in and a knock came at the door to the suite. Angus answered and came back with a bottle of Champagne in an ice bucket and two flute glasses.

They rested one arm over the edge of the tub, a glass of the bubbly in their hand. Annika asked if he had thought any more about Ted Hibbard's offer. He told her he was unsure because he was used to a hands-on role, and he didn't know how he would take to working indoors. She concurred because she knew she loved working with animals and she didn't know if she could take to an administrative role either, but they agreed there was plenty of time to decide.

She moved around to his side of the tub, took a sip of Champagne, and said, "Talking about animals," as her hand went beneath the foam and searched for his groin. As she kissed him, her tongue went deep to the back of his mouth. He responded and ran his hand up her thigh. With his free hand, he rolled her nipple between his fingers.

Annika lifted a leg over his as he slid down in the tub and she took his stiff shaft and slid it inside. As she began to gyrate, he took her nipple in his mouth. He nibbled and sucked one while rolling the other in his fingers. He kissed her deep, sucking at her tongue. Her body began shaking, her orgasm rising as he exploded inside her again.

They clung to each other, breathless, a mixture of water and sweat sticking her breasts to his chest. As their normal breathing returned, he took soap from the dish and began washing her. When he washed between her thighs, she gave an involuntary twitch; she told him either he stopped, or he would only have to wash her again later. He grinned, handed her the soap, and picked another from the dish.

* * *

THEY SAT DINING in the open at the candle-lit table, "This is the only thing I miss," Angus said as he cut another bit size chunk from the rare fillet steak on his plate.

"But we eat well at Nyanga," Lindani responded.

Angus nodded. "I know, but nothing beats a good beef-steak, cooked well in a restaurant." They continued drinking at the table by the poolside drinking until late. He'd had five beers and three glasses of wine with dinner.

"Would you like a kiss of death," he asked Lindani as he ordered himself a whiskey Lindani asked he shook his head and shuddered. "Grapes and barley don't mix." Angus then had to explain to Anashe how wine and whiskey were made, and they didn't mix well.

Besides, they'd had the drive home to Nyanga the next day, well… their home for now. When they retired for the night, Annika lay in the crook of his arm. She told him how she too looked on Nyanga station as her home too. Think about it, had she not been posted there she would have missed out on a new love. He kissed the side of her temple and reached over with his free hand, slipping it between her legs.

She winced. "You've broken me, Angus, no we have broken it."

He sat up. "You're in pain… is it the baby?"

She laughed. "No," she said through a chuckle.

Angus was kneeling on the bed in front of her. "What's the matter then?"

Annika told him she thought their earlier lovemaking had been a bit too intense. She lifted the sheet as if she could look underneath herself. He took the sheet and peeled it back she had her legs open; she was red and swollen.

"It stings," she told him, "but it'll calm down in a few

days." Angus climbed off the bed and he went to the bathroom. She heard him run the taps on the Jacuzzi. The water was only lukewarm and as she sat in the tub alone, her cheeks puffed as she blew with relief. As the cool water eased the sting between her legs, she stayed there for a good five minutes like that, before he ran the hot tap when it became too cold for her. Eventually the stinging subsided. He towelled her down when she got out of the tub, she lay beneath the sheet with her legs spread open and slept like that until the light of dawn filled the room.

When she sat up, he jumped. "What's wrong?"

She smiled. "Nothing," she said through a chuckle.

They washed and dressed and were about to go to breakfast when Angus stopped and held her wrist. He nodded in a sort of downward manner. "Are you Okay?"

She lifted the white loose-fitting dress up to her waist "Yes, all better." When his eyes went to her thighs, he saw she had no pants on. Angus groaned with desire and she chuckled again.

CHAPTER 23

They had breakfast, then packed their luggage inside the Crocodile. Lindani ran the engine with the air conditioning on full, as Angus opened the turret and mounted the Brownings. With the interior of the big truck cooled down, they got out and locked the doors; they went to reception to check out as they handed the room keys to the girl behind the desk, pale face Harry appeared at their side.

"So sorry to see you go gentlemen, please be sure to book the George when you visit Salisbury again." He shook hands with them all as they left for the parking lot "it's amazing the way some people's attitude changes when you threaten to shoot them" Angus said when they reached the Crocodile.

As they threaded their way out-of-town Angus stopped the truck outside a butcher the sign above it said. 'Scottish Butcher'. He climbed down and went inside. Fifteen minutes later he appeared with a little chubby man dressed in a blue and white stripped apron over a white coat. They both carried two cardboard boxes each and Lindani opened the back doors of the truck. They loaded the chilled meat inside.

"Hang on, don't shut the doors yet," Angus told him,

went inside again, and came out with two more boxes. With the doors secure, he climbed back into the driver's seat.

"What did you buy?" Annika asked.

"A taste of Scotland, wait and see," he told her, "you'll love it."

The drive back to Nyanga was uneventful. Dakaria opened the gates to the station as they drove in. He noticed Mandala come out of the surgery, with his R1 held across his chest.

Manodno came to meet them when they'd parked, and Angus climbed down from the cabin. He told him they had caught two poachers after they'd come across an old bull elephant they had killed. They had stalked the poachers for three days until they came back. They usually let the carcass start rotting so they could remove the tusks easier.

"Where are they?"

"We've locked up in two of the animal cages in the surgery. They removed the tusks they were in the surgery as well." Angus headed over to the surgery and looked at the two men locked in the cages."

"You got their weapons?" Angus asked Manodno.

"They're in the main building."

"Good, I'll call the police at Nyanga to come and get them."

Angus went back to the crocodile and drove it across to the skinning station; Annika went with him; she was curious to see what he had bought. He unloaded the boxes and stacked them on a table next to the big wooden cutting block. Taking the first box, he opened it on the block and pulled out little plastic tubs containing a grey pasty looking substance.

"Potted hock" he said with a big grin and took them to the fridge room. He laid them out on a shelf.

"You eat that? She asked, he nodded and grinned without saying anything.

He returned to the block and opened the second box, pulling out eight oblong pink blocks of meat that looked like packed pink mince. "Square slice." The grin came again, as if he had made a major conquest. He took them to the fridge room, stacked them next to the other pots. He repeated this process until the first two boxes were empty. Black pudding, and a whole box of bacon, were more of Angus's favourites.

Annika smiled when at last there was something his wife recognised.

"Don't tell me, these are some kinds of pies."

"Mutton pies," Angus confirmed and took them to the fridge, last box two full fillets of beef.

"What were those grey string of sausages?

"Haggis," he explained it was sheep's intestines, and she shuddered. I'm not kissing you after you eat those.

Angus closed the fridge room door and padlocked it.

She started laughing. "My poor Angus, are you actually going to eat that repulsive stuff?"

He grinned, "It's the Food of the Gods, you wait until you taste it all."

She bent over, pretending to vomit. They got back in the truck and parked it in front of the building. Annika clutched the black velvet box the jeweller had given us in Salisbury, close to her breast. He took her down to the cellar. He opened the ammunition safe and placed it on the bottom shelf at the back.

* * *

AFTER THEY HAD UNPACKED, Annika asked when he was going to tell them the station was being closed. Angus frowned, and he told her he had told Lindani not to say anything as it was his job to tell them. He went to the radio in the office and spoke to Jack Jones about the poachers he told him they would come and get the next day. Angus went to the stoep and asked Manodno to bring him the guns the poachers had with them. When he brought them back, he identified them as two old B S A .303 bolt action rifles probably second world war.

He told Manodno to put them back and tell everyone they would eat on the stoep he later as he had something to tell them. When everyone assembled on the stoep, they all shook hands with him and Annika congratulating on their wedding. They had their wedding celebration with their friends on the stoep; the table laid with meats, roast chickens, vegetables, and fruit. They were treated to more Acapello singing.

The celebrations went on into the dark and after they all retired, Annika lay in bed on her side and Angus snuggled up behind her, his arm over her hip.

"I'm horny," he said.

"I am too tender to do anything about that tonight. But I can pleasure you if you like."

"No, if you can't do it, there was no enjoyment in it for him."

As she drifted off to sleep, she thought what a wonderful loving, caring man she had married. Yannie god rest him, would have made the other choice.

* * *

ANGUS SPENT the morning in the fridge room cutting the fillets of beef, slicing the black pudding and square slice sausage, and wrapping them in small portions with grease-proof paper, and freezing them. He took a portion of potted meat with him to let the others try. On the stoop, he brought some fresh bread from the kitchen.

Annika was not in the surgery as the two prisoners were waiting to be picked up. He took a little portion of the meat and placed it on a bit of bread and asked Annika if she would like to try it; she did but told him it looked awful but tasted lovely, the texture of the meat and the hint of spice. Most African people ate it without hesitation but many of them would never refuse food; either out of respect or knew what hunger was. Jack Jones arrived just before noon with Corporal Nyasha; they congratulated both him and Annika on their marriage. After they had refreshments Jack Jones stood up "right let's see the buggers."

Manodno removed the padlock from the first animal cage and Corporal Nyasha went in and handcuffed the man's hands behind his back and brought him out and the repeated the same with the second man.

They took the two men to the back of the big Ford truck they came in, and Jack Jones opened the cage built on the flat back, he took hold of the first man by the elbow Nyasha took the other elbow and they hoisted him up on to the truck "sit" Jones ordered Nyasha climbed up and secured the man by another maniacal closing it over the chain of the handcuffs, they repeated the procedure with the other man.

They took statements from Manodno and Mandala and said they would be in touch. The men shook hands as they left. They watched the police truck disappear in the dust before he turned to Lindani.

"That's actually a good sign."

"What do you mean?" Lindani asked.

"When the poachers are out, there is never any military activity in the area. I think they have better intelligence than the army, but if they are out again, we need to step up patrols.

* * *

THE WEEKS PASSED with neither poaching nor military activities in the area. Annika's stomach was growing bigger, and most nights he would snuggle into her back as they slept. Their love making was just as intense but less frequent. She preferred being on top or he would take her from behind. Angus had been sleeping with an arm around her, and the baby's movement woke him. Angus jumped and was instantly kneeling on the bed.

"What's wrong?"

"I don't know I was asleep, and something hit my arm."

She smiled at him. "It was the baby kicking, Angus."

He looked shocked, "it wasn't a flutter, it felt like a jolt."

Annika took his hand and placed it on her stomach. "Wait." She told him to wait a few minutes later and when the baby moved again, he instantly pulled his hand away.

"Jesus." he started with the questions how long had it been doing that? Was it due to be born, she told him good movement was a healthy sign that everything was progressing well. He lay down on the bed again. "Now your mum said you have woken me from my sleep, so you'd better think of a way to make me sleepy again."

Annika chuckled, and she rolled on her side with her back to him as she slipped her big maternity pants to her knees and reached down the front of his boxer shorts taking hold of his limp penis as it stiffened. "We can't, I might hurt the baby," she laughed. "Angus, you are well endowed, but you would have to be twice your size to reach the baby." she gripped him and slid him inside her, "go slow." She told him. They were both tired, so it only took minutes until they were both spent and slept like that for what remained of the night.

Next day Chatambuza shouted something in Shona from the fire station on the roof Manodno pointed towards the road dust rose in the air, someone was coming they waited and watched. The crocodile lumbered up through the gates and stopped in front of the steps Ted climbed from the rear this time only a slight wave, not his usual one, he climbed the steps to where Angus stood and shook hands with him; he crossed to where Annika sat her hands clasped on top of her bulging stomach; he stooped and kissed her on the cheek.

He turned his eyes back to Angus "Not good news Angus," he said, "Nyanga came out of the hat." He knew it was a possibility it could be them, but had pushed it to the back of his mind.

"When" he asked.

"Two months." He went on to tell them it was not his decision the directive came from the minister for the Interiors office. "I had no say in the matter, sorry" he told him he did not blame him. "So, there will be no beer for me then,."

Angus called Dova and told her to bring two beers, when she had gone, he told him he would tell the station staff after dinner as it was not fair to leave that to him. Angus thanked him he asked when the baby was due.

"Seven weeks" Annika told him.

"Bad timing," she nodded, have you thought any more about the positions I offered. They told him they had not their thoughts had mostly been concentrated on the baby coming. Ted said now they knew they would have to think hard about what to do. "Where is Lindani?"

Angus shouted for him he came to the stoep. Ted shook his hand "Can you ask your wife to come."

He went away and returned with Anashe. "Have you discussed the option I gave you if Nyanga were to close?

He nodded. "Yes, we have."

Ted looked at him, "And?"

Lindani took a deep breath "I am of the bush Mr Hibbins, I don't know if I could live in a town. I am a tracker."

Ted nodded. "Okay, but I would like you to try the course. If you don't like it or living in the city, I will guarantee you a tracker's post at Matazari." He looked at Anashe and they both nodded. Angus said he would have to tell the others, Ted told him he would do it.

CHAPTER 24

*T*ed asked Lindani to ask them all to come to the stoep. When they were all assembled, he began. He told them the station would be run down over a period of eight weeks before it was to be closed.

"The area will be combined with Matazari station, which will be enlarged to cover both, the breeding program and area protection. Everyone will be transferred there if they wished to continue working. He went on to tell them neither Angus, Annika, Lindani and his wife would be with them as they would be going to Salisbury. He asked if there were any questions.

"What do you mean, run down?" Mandala asked.

"Everything except the buildings will be moved over to Matazari. As Nyanga is closing, the Crocodile is going to Salisbury as the army are requisitioning it." When he had finished talking, they all drifted away, leaving only Angus and Annika on the stoep.

"When do we start?" Angus asked.

"What animals are you holding?"

Annika told him there were only a few; none that are in a

serious condition and couldn't be released within the time period. "We can go around tomorrow and see what has to go and what we can leave" Angus nodded.

Dinner was very brief and solemn that night it seemed everyone had lost their appetites. As Ted ate Angus and Annika picked at the food only Ted had a few beers Angus did not feel like drinking.

Annika was true to her word, and they spent the next morning touring the station. Angus made up an inventory of what would be taken to Matazari. Everything except the buildings would go, even the roof sheeting would be taken off.

When they finished, they sat on the stoop and assessed the workload and timetable; agreeing they should manage it within the eight-week timeline.

"We'll only have the Isuzu to transport everything across, which will slow things down. Every trip would be a day there and a day back."

"That can't be helped as Matazari only have two Land Rovers."

Ted and his driver left at first light, Angus gathered all the men on the stoop, first he told them they would begin dismantling the steel cages in the surgery it would be a slow process as the only had one spanner to fit the bolts at held the panels together and Angus didn't know how easy they would unscrew, they had been built years ago.

At the first try he knew it would not be easy as they tried the first bolt, as it fought against their efforts with creaks at every little turn with the spanner. He told Manodno to bring some engine oil and brake fluid from the workshop; he brushed the stubborn bolt where its threads showed with brake fluid and left it to soak for a minute then tried it again, success it unscrewed easier.

It took the men the rest of the day to dismantle one cage

seven to go; they carried the five sections outside, and then they found out they could only get three sections of the cage on the Isuzu at an angle. Suddenly, eight weeks did not seem long enough. Angus instructed Manodno and Mandala to take the truck to the workshop and pack what they could around the cage sections.

When the truck left for Matazari the next morning; Chatambuza in the driving seat and Banele beside him, he told them to ask for another spanner at Matazari. He and Lindani began removing the air conditioning in the surgery, and Mandala continued dismantling the cages with Dakaria. Meanwhile, Manodno took the high watch post in the main building.

By mid-afternoon he was regretting starting on the air conditioning, the sweat soaked their bodies he should have left it until the cages had been removed. Even with the windows and door open, the air was stale and dry.

When they finished work for the day, they showered the grime from their bodies then sat in the kitchen; the only room in the building with an air conditioning unit and had dinner at the table. They were all exhausted not only by the physical work but also the drain on their bodies. Then he came to the next problem; which two was he going to ask to do night watch? Manodno volunteered and Dova said she would stay awake and Dakaria could sleep beside her.

The problem was solved in the short term, but he knew the winddown was going to be difficult, it was only the first day of being two men down at the station.

They started work again the next morning at first light, an hour later a Dakota flew low over the station heading East. They ran out of the surgery, shielding their eyes as they watched pass.

"Shit" he said to Lindani, "We've been complacent again, we have been too busy here to notice we have no weapons with us." He told them all to bring their weapons and put on their side arms on as well. Fortunately, they had no problem.

Chatambuza and Banele returned mid-afternoon and told them they saw parachutists drop earlier.

"Where?" Angus asked.

"About ten kilometres this side of Nyanga." Angus felt this was too close.

They loaded the Isuzu again with three more cage sections; he told them they would not be going to Matazari the next day if there was the threat of terrorists in the area. He called Jack Jones on the radio after dinner and was informed there had been heavy fighting. The stop group had encountered a big band of terrorists and killed some of them, but the rest had scattered, they were trying to track them.

Angus told Annika he was going to do night watch that night and when she went to bed, he kissed her and told her if anything starts; I want you to get into the Crocodile with Anashe; he had told Lindani he was to make sure she was safe, and he would be on the cannons. Angus felt relieved the vehicle was still at the station.

He went to the roof space and looked out into the darkness over the main door; it was a clear star lit night every few minutes he would scan the area with the starlight scope. All he saw was a Warthog sow and her piglets nosing the ground in the area they had cleared. He sat in silence there in the dark watching them when suddenly she took off running a squealing, her offspring following.

Something had spooked them. A lion or a leopard, he thought, then he saw movement at the edge of the clearing, just movement of the brush. He held his breath as he watched so hard, his vision started to blur. He took the scope away and rubbed his eye.

Looking back through the scope he saw movement again he was concentrating on the ground where it met the brush.

He was about to take the scope from his eye when he the bright green eerie shape of a man's head came into his site. It was still and looking directly towards him.

He lifted his radio and whispered. "Mandala come in," the whisper came back.

"Yes, Angoos?"

"Wake the others. There's movement in front of the main building. Send Banele to wake Lindani and bring Dova and Busani." He looked through the scope again nothing moved.

After a couple of minutes, a figure slowly emerged from the brush, then a second about two meters on his left, they stood at the edge of the clearing looking towards the station. It was night, but in the star lit night it was possible to see the hundred meters ahead of him and make the out their shapes.

The two figures started moving forward slowly, and then another five emerged and started moving slowly across the open ground towards the fence. His radio came to life with a whisper.

"Angoos I have the women and Banele in the Crocodile with me."

Angus whispered back, "Seven men armed in front of the building. Get Banele ready to start the engine, you get on the cannons and wait if it starts fire where you see muzzle flashes."

They were fifty meters from the bush now, and Angus put the scope against the top of the RPD and picked out one of the eerie figures and pressed the trigger. The rattle of the gun split the night, the orange tracers bounced on the hard earth, and went skyward. Banele started the engine, Manodno started strafing the open ground with his RPD, then as they started shooting back Lindani opened up with the Brownings. The muzzle flashes stopped, and it went quiet. The only noise was the diesel engine of the crocodile; he spoke into his radio.

"Lindani tell Banele to turn the engine off." As the engine died, his ears rang with the noise in the confines of the roof space. He looked through the scope three figures lay on the ground there was no sign of the other four. They all spent the rest of the night alert where they were.

The hint of dawn lit the sky stars were still visible he told them all to come to the stoep. "Four of them have escaped they're going in pursuit. Manodno and Mandala stay here with Banele and the women get something to eat and drink, then all of you in the back of the crocodile stay there until we get back."

Angus, Lindani, Chatambuza, Dakaria and the ridge-backs, they went past the three bodies lying beyond the fence: the dogs sniffing the ground. When they picked up the spoor, they started tracking though the thick bush.

They had gone about four kilometres when the dogs stopped and looked at Lindani, then back to the bush.

"They're close spread out ten meters straight line."

They started moving slowly forward through the thick brush until they'd gone about three hundred meters when they heard a loud metallic snap followed by the blast from the ten-bore gun. Dakaria had been moving forward and he'd stood on the trigger plate of a big poachers, gin trap. It snapped shut across his shin; the pain caused his finger to squeeze the trigger on the Argyle as he fell to the ground.

As he opened his eyes, the four camouflaged men were nearly on him. He fired the Argyle. The heavy bullet hit the first one in the head, exploding it, he fired again the shot from the other ten bore barrel hit another in the chest; it was a greased round; it tore most of his right shoulder and chest away. The guy went backwards, knocking the third man who was behind him as he fell to the ground. He pulled the trigger again and nothing happened it was empty. The man remaining standing smiled and drew a panaga, as he moved toward lifting the big blade above his head. He was knocked from his feet in a flash as the two sixty-kilogram ridgeback dogs slammed into him simultaneously. They sent him tumbling and screaming as they started to savage him. Two shots rang out as the last of the four got to his feet, and sent him back to the ground, Lindani shouted the dogs off the now bloodied figure on the ground, and his face was torn away.

Landani went to the bodies he had used the Argyle on big animals, but it was the first time he saw the damage they could cause to a human. The .460 bullet had hit the man in the head there was nothing from the bridge of his nose up. The top of his head was gone, the other who had been hit by the greased shot had most of his torso and shoulder torn away. As the men collected the weapons from the bodies, Lindani let out a shout: Oh! No... Oh! No. As he fell to his knees looking at the body of the man who had taken the ten-bore blast. He pointed to the mutilated body.

"What's wrong? Angus said, "What is it?"

It is the body of Anashe's husband, my brother."

Angus came over to him. "Are you sure?"

Lindani nodded. "How could he? How could he attack his own wife, his own family?" He spat at the corpse.

They used two of their AK-47 rifles to prise open the strong gin trap from Dakaria's leg Angus wrapped the open wound with a strip he tore from his shirt.

They took it in turns to carry him to the station; they eventually covered the four kilometres sweat soaked and took him to the surgery. Annika dressed his leg and reset the break as best she could but said to Angus he will need to go to a doctor, as it was a crush break there may be bone fragments, she could not plaster it but secured it with splints and bandage.

Angus told Chatambuza to take him to Matazari with his

wife, Banele and his wife as well, there not enough room in the truck cab so Banele sat on the roof of the cage with an R1 as they passed through the gates. When they had gone, they headed for the stoep, Angus told Manodno to bring Anashe to them, Annika was already on the stoep when he and Lindani arrived.

"What happened?" he screwed his eyes and gave a slight shake of his head. Anashe came on the stoep. Lindani told her to sit down, and he sat beside her.

"When was the last time you spoke to Bukhosi?" She studied his expression.

"Why?" she asked. He gripped her upper arms, "just tell me." Her eyes were wide.

"After your last visit; he went to gather wood for the cooking fire". "And you never saw him again? She shook her head "Why what is it, Lindani?"

He took a deep breath and said almost in a whisper. "We killed him today," she threw her hands to her face. "Anashe, he was one of the men who attacked us last night." Her hands came from her face. "He was a terrorist?" He nodded.

"I didn't know Lindani, believe me." He embraced her. "I do, Anashe". As they sat in a silent embrace Lindani said, "Anashe you don't have to be my wife any longer, the man who took you for his wife is no brother of mine."

She broke from the embrace as Angus and Annika got up and left the stoep. "You don't want me as your wife?"

Lindani shook his head. "I do not mean it that way, I mean now I have disowned my brother, you do not have to commit to me."

She was silent for a moment then asked, "Can I stay as your wife?"

He moved his face to hers and kissed her. "I would like that."

* * *

THEY WERE down to four men now. But that day they didn't work, the chase and the firefight with its result had drained them all emotionally. They spent the day resting. When night came, Angus put a cot in to the back of the Crocodile, Annika and Anashe slept in there, while he had the Brownings, Lindani in the roof space with the scope and RPD. Annika was very quiet as she sat on the stoop, her hands clasped on top of her bulge. Angus could see she was worried when she looked at him.

"I am scared, Angus."

He sat beside her and put his arm around her shoulder. "You're not the only one, Annika. If I could turn the clock back, I would never have come here."

She looked at him. "Then I would never have met you," he told her he didn't mean it in that way. She told him he knew what he meant, but still she was afraid.

"I thought nothing else mattered when I lost Yannie, I didn't care what happened to me, sometimes I wished I was dead as well." Angus hugged her and told her he had felt the same when his wife had died.

"Don't you ever say that again, don't even think it, I love you."

The night passed painfully slow a slight breeze blew it did not help, Lindani was constantly scanning the area with the scope late into the night he saw a movement, they came out of the brush one after another six female lions with four cubs and a big male. The alpha female, her head high sniffing the breeze, she had the scent of the three bodies lying on the open ground. The male with a huge mane broke in to trot and pounced on one body. The females and cubs went to the other two and started feeding.

Angus relaxed; if anyone was coming tonight, he would

187

not be their only worry. The lions had just settled when he noticed further movement coming from the brush, a pack of Hyenas. They made their way straight to where the lions were feeding and pestered them; darting in, trying to get at the carrion they were feeding on.

To his surprise, he felt no sympathy for the men who were now only that carrion, he never thought he would sit and watch them feed on humans.

Everyone was now awake with the noise of roars and yaps from the joust going on beyond the fence. A pack of wild dogs had joined the party now, and they contributed to the din. Lindani came to the rear of the Crocodile and told them what was going on Anashe took it in her stride she was African, she asked who wanted a cup of coffee as she headed for the kitchen.

Angus radioed to Manodno and told him they were going to have coffee and invited him, and Mandala could come over if they wanted. They all sat in the kitchen with the doors closed to cut the noise level of the symphony from the front out.

They would get no more sleep tonight Angus looked at the wall clock five minutes past three, two and half hours till daybreak. There would be little, or no work, done again today, the noise abated just the stars started to fade in the dawn, they only had fruit for breakfast.

All the men went to the surgery. It was a cloudy day so it would be cooler, and they were not so security conscious because the pride of lions would be lying up sleeping somewhere close by and the Hyena pack would be prowling the area.

They managed to dismantle two cages by the time Chatambuza came back afternoon, he had another man beside him; he introduced him, and his name was Tongia he was one of the flushers from Matazari he would travel back and forth with Chatambuza.

They loaded the truck with another three panels Tongia asked why they didn't tie more on top of the cage. They looked at each other they had only thought of putting them in the cage; they loaded another two on top and tied them down tight a whole cage on one trip. Angus told Annika the cages would be gone in another five trips; she was quiet he asked if she was ok? She told him she was exhausted with the little sleep she had the night before she slept on the cot in the back of the Crocodile gain that night. Next morning, she told him she was going to sleep in their bed again; the cot was making her back ache.

CHAPTER 25

By the end of the first month, the surgery was dismantled and was being transported to Matazari piece by piece. Annika didn't walk any more she waddled the once flat stomach was now bulging; she sat on the stoop most days with her hands clasped on top of the bulge.

She was constantly tired; her hair had lost its shine and her suntan had faded she had developed strange cravings. First it was Angus's potted hock when she had worked her way through the two dozen pots then she started on his mutton pies. He joked with her, telling her the baby would have a Scottish accent like Morton's.

When Angus woke in the dark, Annika was sitting on the edge of the bed clutching her stomach. He got out of the bed and went around to the side she sat on. Tears were running down her cheeks.

"What's wrong," he asked, alarmed.

His wife shook her head. "I don't know, can you ask Anashe tocome?" Angus knocked on Lindanis door and he opened it.

"Aneshe can you see Annika she's not feeling well."

He went to the stoep and left Anashe with her Lindani joined him on the stoep and asked what was wrong; he told him he didn't know. Fifteen minutes later Anashe came and told him Annika wanted to see him. He went to the bedroom while Lindani and Aneshe went back to bed. His wife was still sitting on the edge of the bed.

She told him she'd had a show.

"What's that?"

She explained it was a plug that could indicate the baby will come early.

"What can we do?"

Annika told him she was going to need medical attention, or she might lose the baby; it was seven weeks from her due date.

He went back to Lindani's room and knocked on the door again. Lindani was asked if he would haelp to get her to Salisbury and take her to the hospital. He asked if Anashe accompany him with Annika. Lindani said he would come as well, but Angus told him he would have to stay at the station as the station would be vulnerable with only three men to defend it.

Lindani reminded him Chatambuza and Tongia were due to return from Matazari later that day. If they left at first light, he would come with them and come back again after dropping them at the hospital. Angus agreed, and he went and put a cot in the back of the Crocodile with a blanket and four iced water bottles. Lindani went to the roof space where Manodno was on night watch and told him what they were doing.

"No work today, just be alert," Angus tells him.

With Annika on the cot, they set off just before first light Lindani at the wheel Anashe beside Annika and him in the turret.

The sun had just cleared the horizon when they turned on the main Salisbury road, they could make better speed than they had on the rough road to the camp.

They had been travelling about half an hour when they came to a long sweeping bend in the road as they cleared the bend; they saw four men in green camouflage digging a hole in the middle of the road. They were laying a landmine.

Lindani pressed the triggers and the two Browning barrels spat flame as they sent their deadly load. He fired four short bursts. The road around the men erupted as the heavy projectiles struck in and around them. Lindani braked to a crawl.

Three of them lay dead in the road, the fourth vanished into the bush. Lindani gave another three bursts around the point he had entered the brush.

It seemed surreal to him a sheet of orange flame and curling black smoke shot skyward and a split second later the shockwave came. He must have been the one carrying the landmine. Lindani accelerated again he heard him shout to Anashe they were safe, she had screamed when he stared firing the noise of the guns was deafening and the hot brass cartridge cases fell inside and bounced around.

* * *

THEY ARRIVED at the King Edward infirmary just after ten o'clock. Angus wanted Lindani and him to carry her Annika in on the cot, but she insisted on walking. He told Lindani to go to the department stores and refill the Crocodile with supplies and head back to Nyanga.

He paced the corridor when the nurse took Annika into an examination room. A doctor with a stethoscope over his white-coated shoulder followed where they went moments later. Twenty minutes passed when the nurse came and told him he could see his wife. She held the door open for him. The first room they entered was empty. The nurse passed him and opened another door off the examination room.

Annika had her feet propped up on something under a blanket and a drip on a stand beside the bed its tube was taped to her left wrist.

He asked the nurse what was wrong. She smiled reassuringly and told him, Annika was dehydrated and had an iron deficiency.

"What about the baby?"

"The babies are fine," she said.

"Babies? What babies?"

He looked at Annika she gave him a weak smile, "Twins Angus, we are having twins." He smiled but didn't know what he felt.

The nurse told him his wife needed rest and the doctor would speak to him at evening visiting time. She explained he could only have five minutes alone with his wife, then he would have to come back in the evening.

After she had gone, he went to the bed, kissed her, then sat on the chair beside her bed, and held her hand.

"I told you, Angus. The amount of your seed you put in me it would be a litter of children." they both laughed.

A short time later, the nurse stuck her head around the door and told him had to leave. He went outside into the sunshine and it suddenly dawned on him all he had to wear was what he stood up in. In his haste to leave Nyanga, he had packed no clothes. He headed for the bank and withdrew five hundred dollars. He called Ted and told him he was in town and Annika was in the hospital, Ted met him there at visiting time.

Next, he called the George Hotel. The receptionist confirmed they had a room free and booked it for him. After doing some clothes shopping, he jumped into a taxi and headed to the hotel. When he arrived at the reception desk, it was the same girl as his last visit. As she handed him the room, key pale faced Harry appeared with his false smile.

"Good to have with us again sir, is madam with you?"

He told him she was in hospital the headed for the lift. The room he had been allocated was the one he had on his first visit with Annika. He showered and changed, then had a lunch of chicken salad and two bottles of Castle beside the pool. He felt guilty enjoying himself when his wife was lying in hospital. When he finished eating, he asked the receptionist if he could have a call at six o'clock. Stripping off in his room, he turned the air conditioning to medium and fell asleep in his boxers.

The telephone rang at six and he thanked the receptionist and asked if he could order a taxi for seven o'clock. He showered again then got dressed then spent the next twenty minutes pacing the foyer. The taxi came to a halt outside the hospital five minutes before seven; he asked the driver if he could pick him up again at five past eight and went inside.

There were other people waiting to see friends or family in the corridor. The matron stood at doors that led to the wards, looking at her watch pinned on her chest in one hand, a little bell in the other. At exactly seven o'clock she rang the bell. He went to the room Annika was in she had her head propped up with her pillows her feet were still raised beneath the blanket, colour had begun to return to her face she was smiling. He went to her and kissed her.

She started telling him how they would have to buy two of everything. They would fill the back of the Crocodile, she joked, and the years of pleasure they would have with both each other now with an instant family.

Ted knocked on the room door at seven forty. He got up from her side and let him in. He went to her and kissed her on the cheek, asking how she was. Before she could answer,

Angus announce it was twins. He congratulated her and bent over kissing her cheek again, then turned and shook Angus's hand.

"You've got you work cut out now," he told them.

He only stayed five minutes making his excuses and kissed her cheek again, Ted was discreet about giving them time to themselves.

A few minutes before eight he told her how strict the matron had been at the start of visiting time and warned Annika, she would probably be the same at the end. He kissed her, which was supposed to be a peck on the lips, but she thrust her tongue into his mouth. He stood up. "Annika not I here, I mean it's a hospital."

She started laughing. "I'm horny, Angus," just to watch his reaction. "Now I am teasing," she added.

At that the door opened it was the doctor who had seen her earlier. He told them there was nothing to worry about, but he would prefer to keep Annika in hospital until her situation stabilised, suggesting a week should be enough. Ted was waiting for him at the main entrance. "I think you need a drink, lad." Angus nodded they went to a bar along the road from the hospital.

He asked how long Annika was going to be in hospital; he told him the doctor had said a week. They drank three beers, and he told Ted about the last attack on the station and how Annika told him she was scared.

He thought for a few minutes, then told Angus he could bring the closure forward. He and Annika could come to Salisbury because a station down in the Bulawayo area only had three weeks to run. He could arrange for the warden from there to finish at Nyanga.

He went on to say he would look for a place for them to stay, and if he didn't find one, they could stay at his place. He had three spare rooms in his bungalow. Angus nodded in agreement.

"Speak with Annika before you agree," Ted told him.

He got a taxi back to his hotel and when to the bar, pale face Harry was sitting on a bar stool at the bar. Angus sat at a table and ordered a beer when it came, he said to the server, "Back on the Rouge?" Naming the beer, he had served him with the gold elephant head with spread ears on the black label.

Pale face Harry came with a drink in his hand and sat down opposite him. He asked how his wife was he told him she was stable, and they had just found out she was having twins.

Harry waved the server over. "Bring us Glenmorangie, two glasses and just leave the bottle," he told him.

Angus said he didn't want to get drunk as he did last time when he drank it."

Harry said just one then," holding the bottle. He poured a free measure; they didn't use optics. Harry told him he came from York and had come to Rhodesia fifteen years before when he was eleven with his parents. His father was an engineer and had worked on steam train repairs in the shed at York when they'd lived there.

He explained he couldn't find a job now that the railways had all but shut down due to the war. He then told him he was supporting his father and mother, who lived with him and his wife.

"My wife, Denise is Van-Rooyens sister. I don't like him. Don't tell him I told you that." Angus nodded.

More beers arrived automatically, and Angus stood up to go to the toilet. "Whoa." The room was spinning. He steadied himself by grabbing the back of a chair. "I think it's a pee for me Harry, then bed."

Harry wasn't fairing any better. His head was down, chin

on his chest like it was too heavy to old up anymore. He looked up; eyes glazed. "What? Oh, right," he managed before his eyes shut tight.

Angus made it to the toilets. Doing a dance as he fought with his zipper. Thankfully, he made it. After leaving the toilet he took the lift to his room, threw himself clothed on the bed and passed out.

He woke late into the morning with a cleaner standing in the doorway; but she hadn't opened it. He hadn't closed it the night before. She asked if she should come back, and he nodded. After showing, he felt nearly human and went to have breakfast downstairs. As he ate, he thought what was he going to do to pass the day until visiting time, he only knew Ted in Salisbury. He walked around town and thought he had never felt so lonely, yet Annika was only three kilometres away, but he could not get to her. Not until seven o'clock tonight.

He passed the cinema he had taken Annika to on their first visit to Salisbury together. He looked at the advertising board 'The Deer Hunter' was playing it started at two o'clock.

Half an hour later he went to a nearby café, had a coffee and ham salad sandwich, and watched the world go by. At two p.m. he settled in the cinema seat as the lights dimmed.

The film was not what he expected he thought it was about deer hunting but it was a war film; it started to feel too close to home and made him feel uneasy, so he got up again and left. On his way back to the hotel he stopped at a florist and bought a bunch of flowers, then few other things from various shops.

At the hotel he filled the wash-hand basin and stood the flowers in the water. He showered again and changed his clothes and went to the reception and asked to have the safe opened. Pale face Harry took him to the safe and opened it.

The movie had unsettled him. He took out his Glock 9-millimetre pistol and holster. He undid his belt and put the holster on, so it positioned at his back under his shirt.

Five minutes to eight he was pacing the corridor outside Annika's room. He held butch of flowers in his arm a bag of fruit in his hand, a bottle of concentrated juice and some magazines in the other.

The matron stood with her little bell in hand; her posture made him think she wouldn't have much compassion towards anyone that was sick.

Exactly eight o'clock by her watch she rang the bell, he opened the door to be greeted by a different Annika, colour had come back to her face and her hair shone once again. The drip had been removed she smiled and told him she felt a lot better; he stooped and kissed her then sat on the chair beside the bed.

He held her hand and asked if the doctor had said any more. She'd had some tests and taken blood samples this morning, and the doctor told her he would have the results in few days.

"How would you feel if Ted got someone else to finish running Nyanga down and we could stay in Salisbury?"

"Could we? I'd prefer that to going back there."

"Ted offered to put us up at his place."

"I don't know about that part," she replied warily. Nevertheless, she told him to pass on her thanks.

"What have you been doing today?"

"I was bored. I realised I don't know anyone apart from Ted Hibbins."

"Why don't you pass your time house hunting? If we're going to stay here, you should start looking."

Angus leaned forward and kissed her. "Never thought of that, it's a brilliant idea. Beauty and brains."

She smiled "what more could you ask for?"

He kissed her again, but passionately this time in his arms. He wrapped his arms around her and thought how good she tasted as their tongues slid against each other. A sudden cough sounded it the room, he jumped back.

It was the matron. "I have to take your temperature." he stood back from the bed to let her work; the felt like a teen who had been caught by his mother and stared at the floor. When she finished checking his wife over, she wrote something on the chart hanging on the end of her bed.

"Angus, you're doing it again," Annika said.

"What?"

"looking shy and awkward."

He shrugged "If she'd come in a few minutes later, she would have thought it was me who had a fever."

She laughed. "What do you mean?"

"I was getting hot and not in a sweaty way."

The bell started ringing in the corridor. "That can't be an hour already," he complained.

He told her how much he missed her and took her in his arms again with a lingering deep kiss.

"Did you not hear the bell?" The matron asked. They broke off their embrace and he turned his head. She stood holding the door open, one hand on the door the other on her hip. He smiled at her as he passed and waved at his smiling wife as went through the door.

He walked back to the hotel, stopping at newsagent. He bought a copy of The Evening Standard, sat in the lounge bar when he got back and studied the newspaper with the Headlines. 'Smith in Talks With ZANU and ZAPU. so, Ted's rumours are now fact. He scanned the advertisements in the property section; there were a lot of properties to let. He planned in his head to get in touch with some in the morning and possibly view some.

He decided he would not drink any more tonight.

Against his own advice, left the hotel after deciding to go for a walk. He wandered heading for nowhere in particular some shops had their windows lit he stopped and browsed the goods in the windows.

He was looking in the window of a double fronted furniture shop as his thoughts had turned to setting up a home. They had no furniture of their own, as when he and Morag came to Nyanga everything they needed was there.

In the window's reflection his attention was drawn to a car slowing down the going a little further down the road before doing a U turn and coming back towards him. He reached under his shirt and gripped the butt of the pistol, the car slowed again as it came towards him.

"Thought it was you," he stooped to get a view inside the car Sandy Ewan and Jimmy McGovern.

They asked him what he was doing in Salisbury and he told them about Annika being in hospital. They drove him back to the hotel, telling him they were on leave. Angus invited them in for a drink. As they sat at the table McGovern picked up the newspaper and read the front page. "Looks like it's get out time."

"What do you mean?"

Sandy told him they would get out of Rhodesia if they took over the government, the place would end up in turmoil.

McGovern joked, "I'll have to look around for another war."

"Where will you go?"

"South Africa," Ewan said, "my wife's there. I didn't want to just walk away and leave the house, we bought here, but no one is buying, and we sunk all our money into it. I'll see if I can get a job down there and get enough to get us back to Scotland."

McGovern said he would go south as well and get a flight from Johannesburg back home.

"I'm getting too old for another war," he confessed.

Ewan asked him how Angus was passing his time during the day. He told them he had been bored but was going house hunting during the day, starting the next day.

Ewan told him if he wanted any help or transport, he'd be happy to run him around. "It'll keep me out the pubs." He telephoned a few of the house advertisements and arranged to meet two; one at half past ten, and the other at three o'clock.

The following morning, he walked to nearby newsagents and asked if he could buy a map of the city. The saleswoman told him to go to the city hall. They had them there and would give him one. When the young woman gave him the map, he took out the piece of paper he had written the addresses on and asked her to mark them on the map.

He hailed a cab and told the driver the first address, which was only ten minutes from the city centre. The house was in a cul-de-sac at the end of a treelined road. He asked the driver to wait for him. He went to the door on the stoop; it had a fly screen, and the door was open, Angus called out, and a woman appeared from a door on the right. He asked if she was the person; he had spoken to earlier that morning. She told him she was as she pushed the fly screen open, she held out her hand "Mrs Renshaw," she said, "call me Jan." She noticed the taxi waiting and told him she would take him back to town if he wanted.

He went back to the road and paid the driver off. Jan showed him around the house room by room; four bedrooms and two bathrooms, one en-suite, a large airy lounge with French doors to the rear gardens, and the kitchen had all the white goods. He told her he liked it and asked when the furniture would be moved out, it was to be let furnished, he wouldn't have to wait and furnish it.

She asked if he would like a cold drink and made her way back to the kitchen, Angus followed her she poured orange juice in to two glasses and led the way to the lounge. She told him the gardener came once a week, the garbage collection was every Thursday, and the post box was only a five-minute walk away. Angus decided he would take it. The rent would be a hundred and fifty dollars a month. He gave her the first month's rent and asked who owned it; she told him she did, but she worked at Brady barracks and had a room there.

"I don't come here much since my husband died."

Angus didn't ask how; he didn't want to know. Just stood as she picked up her car keys. He took his wallet out again and gave her a further three hundred dollars, so he paid the rent upfront for three months.

He told her about Annika on the drive back to town. After she dropped him at the hotel, he called the three o'clock appointment and cancelled. He asked for Pale Face Harry at the reception desk and asked him if he knew any good car dealers. He recommended McCarthy's on Victoria Street and gave him directions.

Angus found the car lot with no trouble. McCarthy turned out to be a nice Canadian man who showed him what he had to offer. Angus settled on a white Chrysler Valiant Charger. He wanted twelve hundred dollars for it; he offered nine fifty eventually they shook hand on one thousand dollars.

He came back half an hour later and handed over the money and drove the car back to the parking lot, pale face Harry asked if he found it, he held the keys up to him. When Harry had finished scrutinising it, he gave it his seal of approval. "One beer" he said.

Angus frowned. "What?"

"I did you a favour and now you own me a beer."

When they finished the beer, Angus went to his room. It was still only five o'clock; three hours until visiting time. He had a nap on top of the bed then showered, got dressed. Angus went to the restaurant and ordered a fillet steak and salad, with a jug of fresh orange juice. He parked on the street just along from the hospital and paced the corridor again in same procedure at seven o'clock on the dot.

Annika smiled as he came into the room. He went to her and kissed her and sat beside her, her skin glowed again, she was looking well. "How are feeling today?" he asked.

"A lot better I think the rest is helping me." he noticed her feet were now on the bed, whatever it was under her ankles had gone.

"I rented a house for us today, I hope you'll like it… oh, and a car." Angus took the map from his pocket and pointed to where it was and gave her a description of it. He felt better about visiting her tonight, they had something to talk about. He told her of the conversation he had with Ewan and McGovern.

"Things must be getting serious if people are thinking like that. I heard in on the news about the talks at noon."

He nodded "What radio?" she pointed at a transistor radio on the bedside cabinet.

"Where did that come from?" She told him the nurse brought it in that morning. It had been handed in at reception by Ted.

"He's still after you," he laughed.

The door opened, and the matron put her head in. "The bell will go in five minutes," she announced, then closed it again. They laughed.

"She's got your number, McLean."

Angus leaned over and kissed her.

Annika winced. "What's wrong?" She shifted position on

the bed. "Probably nothing. One of the babies moving or something."

The bell sounded, and he kissed her again. "See you tomorrow, I love you."

He got back to the hotel there was a message for him; Ted wrote the note asking him to come to the office next day, there was something he had to discuss with him.

He went to bed and lay listening to South African Broadcasting, a show where they call people up, pretending to be an official department with a complaint against them. It was a prank show, and it cheered him up. He turned the radio off at ten and fell asleep.

Next morning, he headed for the department offices after breakfast. Ted came down as soon as the receptionist told him he was here.

In his office, Hibbard told him the warden he was talking about would not be available for another three weeks… "I know this is a big ask, but how would you feel about going back to Nyanga until he is available?"

He thought for a moment. "I'll have to speak to Annika about it."

Ted smiled. "You're learning, lad."

Angus told him Ted he had rented a house over on Sunny Ridge and had bought a car

"You're all set then."

When Angus left Ted, he took a drive out to Brady barracks. He asked the guard at the gate if he could find out if Sandy Ewan was on the base. The soldier studied a list held together with a bulldog clip board. He had a nasal Liverpool accent.

"Erm ees not gone out today, mate." Angus asked if he could see him. The guard lifted the telephone and spoke to someone, then put the handset back in its cradle. "Just ang on ere mate".

Angus smiled when he saw Ewan coming towards the guardroom, crossing the parade ground in his civvies, a pair of denim shorts and a yellow tee shirt.

In the guardroom, Ewan shook his hand. "You need a lift?"

"No, I've bought a car. I just thought I'd see what you were up to."

Ewan shrugged "Nothing much. You?"

Angus told him he had rented the house in Sunny Ridge. "I'm heading over there and thought you could tag along."

"I suppose it's better than staying in there all day," he replied, nodding towards the barracks.

Once in the car, the Valiant made its way across the city.

Ewan slapped the dashboard. "How are you going to get fuel for this Vee six, isn't it? Petrol is rationed two four gallons a week."

Angus nodded. "Government employee special dispensation," he replied as he turned onto the driveway.

"Nice," said Ewan, inspecting the front of the building. "Much better than the barracks."

Angus took him on a tour of the house. "All the comforts of home, eh?"

Angus' mind wandered back to Nyanga. That was his home for the past three years and nine months. Now it was being denied him. "Hello." Ewan said.

"Sorry, I was miles away," Angus said.

"Did you know Nyanga station was closing? Ewan told him he knew some stations were being closed, but not which ones.

"What are me and my men going to do for a beer now," he joked.

"What are you and Annika going to do?"

"They have offered me Deputy Head of Department, and Annika; head of veterinary, here in Salisbury."

He raised his eyebrows and nodded. "And your accepting?"

He told him they would try it but had another option if it didn't work out.

"But at least we will be here when Annika gives birth." As they headed back into the city, Ewan asked if would mind if he came along to visit Annika. Angus he told him she would probably be glad of the extra company as they struggled for conversation on some visits. He dropped him back at the barracks and arranged to pick him up again at six thirty.

Back in the hotel he told pale face Harry he would be checking out tomorrow. He'd paid for a house so he thought he should move in and make the place ready for Annika when she got out of the hospital. They arrived to visit Angus's wife at five minutes to seven. When they reached the corridor outside Annika's room, Ted was already waiting, a bunch of mixed flowers in his hand.

"Hope you don't mind me visiting," he said. Angus shook his head when the matron rang the bell; both men told him they would give him some time alone with Annika.

When they entered the room, she was reading one of the magazines he'd brought for her. She lowered it and smiled. "Hello, darling," she said.

Angus bent and kissed her. "It is a long day sitting here. I'm as bored as hell. The only people I see are the nurses when they come to take my temperature or bring my food."

He told her he had other visitors with him tonight, and he was moving into the house the next day. He also told her he had taken Sandy Ewan to see it and he liked it.

Quarter of the visiting time had gone by the time he went to the door and waved in Sandy and Hibbard. Ewan shook her hand and told her how well she looked, Ted didn't shake her hand, he just held it, stooped and kissed her on the cheek.

As they chatted Angus sat on the edge of the bed, Ted sat

in the chair and Sandy stood. After ten minutes the door opened, and the matron strode in.

"Only two visitors," she said, throwing her gaze to the ceiling.

Sandy said he would wait by the car. Angus threw the keys to him as he left. When they were alone, Ted told Annika what he had discussed with Angus that morning.

She looked undecided, "But Ted, Angus is the only visitor I have most days."

He nodded. "I'm sorry I had to ask. I'll see if I can sort something else out." He stood, not long afterwards and left.

After he had gone, Annika suddenly said. "The diamonds Angus where are they?"

He told her they were still at Nyanga that was the last thing he had on his mind when they left.

"Then you must go back." He hadn't thought about them, he had been more concerned about her and the baby... babies.

"Our passports and wedding papers are there as well," she told him. He nodded just as the bell rang. "I'll tell Ted tomorrow." Angus stood and hugged her. "I'll go back the day after tomorrow." He kissed her again and left.

In the corridor a voice behind him said quietly, "Mister McLean." He turned and saw it was the doctor he'd seen when he brought Annika in.

"Yes?"

"Can I have a word with you?" He pointed to a door off the corridor.

His heart pumped fast in his chest. What's wrong? In the side room, the doctor told him he would like to keep Annika in hospital until the babies were born.

"She never mentioned it to me, "he said.

"No, I haven't told her. I wanted to ask you first."

"I am not the patient you should have told Annika first."
They went across to Annika's room.

When the doctor told her, she looked at Angus. "Whatever is best for our babies."

He asked the doctor if she had to stay in the side ward
could she not be moved to a general ward? The doctor told
them he didn't see why not? As he drove back, he told Sandy
he was going back to Nyanga the day after tomorrow.

"Don't drive me back to the barracks, park this up at your
hotel, and we will have a drink." When their drinks arrived,
he told him what the doctor had told them at the hospital.

"Might be for the best," Sandy agreed.

ANGUS WAS at the department reception desk before Ted
arrived for the day's work he stood from the sofa as he came
through the doors. When they reached his office, he told him
what the doctor had told them at the hospital the night
before, and that he would go back to Nyanga until this
replacement arrived.

Ted nodded and told him to come back early the next
morning and transport would take him. He asked if it would
be ok if Anashe came back with the transport provided
Lindani agreed she could stay at the house.

Hibbard agreed and then asked if it would be alright if he
visited Annika while he was at Nyanga?

"She would be glad of the company." Angus told him and
could he take anything she wanted to her. Ted said he would.

On his way back to the hotel something came to him. He
would have to buy a case or a duffle bag he had nothing to
put his belongings in. As he went through the foyer, pale face
Harry told him his bill was ready; he forgot he said he was
leaving that day. He told him he had a change of plan he was

going back up country the next day and would need the room for one more night.

He left to go to the hospital a little early and walked along the rows of shops until he came to one that sold bags. After purchasing a sports bag, he made his way to see his wife. When he reached corridor outside her room, he realised he didn't know if Annika had been moved to a general ward.

Seeing a nurse, he stopped her and asked where Annika was. She pointed to a pair of double doors with green curtains drawn across the glass panels. A sign fixed to the wall next to the doors told him it was the maternity ward.

"She's not in labour?" he said in a panic. "No, but it is where she will stay until the babies are born."

The ward's main lights were off, but there were reading lights above the six beds, set in two rows of three, facing each other. He spotted her in the last bed in the line by the window and smiled. She was sitting on an armchair beside the bed reading a magazine when he walked up beside her. She looked up and smiled.

"How are you feeling today, darling? He asked as he rounded the bed he stooped and kissed her first on the cheek then on the lips. "I feel great. I asked the doctor when he came on his rounds today if it was necessary for me to stay here in hospital. I told him we'd rented a house.

"And?"

"He told me I needed complete rest and the only way I can get it is in here."

He nodded. "He thinks it might have been the stress of the events at Nyanga that started my condition."

"No doubt," Angus agreed.

"How are you liking it here in the ward?"

She smiled. "It's much better than being stuck I that room on my own."

She pointed towards another woman further down the ward.

"She's lovely, that's Carine Laroy. She came from Hilversum, which is only fifteen kilometres away from where I lived in Utrecht, in the Netherlands.

"Small world." he smiled.

"She told me she had the same problem as me with her first baby, but it turned out fine in the end." Angus felt thankful for the woman's reassurance to his wife. He leaned forward and kissed her on the lips as he sat on the edge of her bed.

A cough came from behind him. Angus turned, and the matron stood with her hands on her hips.

"The beds are for the patients NOT for the visitors" she scowled then turned and marched off.

"She should be in the bloody army. She would stop the insurgents from coming over the border." Annika threw her head back and laughed.

They continued to talk, and Angus told her Ted asked if could visit while he was at Nyanga. She said that would be nice of him.

"I still think he's after you," he laughed.

"Well, you'd better not stay away to long Angus McLean. Tell everyone at Nyanga I was asking for them and send my love to them." he nodded and eyed the clock at the end of the ward above the doors.

"Any minute now," he said.

Annika stood up and hugged him tightly.

"Please be very careful, Angus, I love you and we need you," she said, rubbing her bump as her eyes welled with tears. He kissed her and it was a lingering one so that she didn't see the tears in his eyes as well.

The bell rang as they parted at the doors he turned and waved to her blowing her a kiss and he left. Annika lay awake long into the night, thinking how much her life had changed in the past eighteen months. She had been happily married to Yannie now he was gone. She had been happy at Nyanga now that to was gone too. She could have lost the babies. She prayed she wouldn't lose Angus as well.

CHAPTER 26

*A*ngus parked the Chrysler in the visitors' parking bay outside the department offices at eight o'clock the following morning. Ted walked into the parking area just as the news came on the car radio. There had been heavy fighting overnight at Mutare, and the broadcaster said the military were currently engaging major insurgency forces. Mutare was a hundred kilometres south of Nyanga, no great distance in Africa.

Ted came over to the Chrysler "Ready to go?" he asked.

Angus nodded and grabbed the holdall from the passenger seat and locked the car door.

"Ted, do you drive?"

"Yes, but I haven't bothered to have a car living in the city."

He tossed him the car keys. "You might as well use this until I get back."

Ted smiled. "Thanks, it'll save me using taxis when I visit Annika."

He asked Angus how she was, and Angus explained her

mood was better since she'd been moved to the maternity ward now.

The big Crocodile vehicle came rumbling into the car park and Angus got ready to leave. "Take care of yerself, lad," Ted said as they shook hands. He nodded and climbed on board.

* * *

As THEY PASSED Epworth on the Mutare road, the houses got scarcer as the city gave way to the dense bush. From there it was sixty kilometres to Marondera, the next human habitat. There was very little traffic on the road. Marondera comprised of not much more than a few stores, a few houses, and a collection of Rondavels with their round red mud walls and thatched roofs. They had only passed two trucks and one car going in the opposite direction.

Seventy kilometres on they come to Rusape, where they would leave the Mutare road and head due east towards the station. Again, the traffic was light.

When they reached Rusape, it was noon. The sun was directly overhead and so they stopped for lunch. After freshening up in the toilets, they had Sadza which meant rolling the cornmeal into a ball between their fingers and dipping it in sauces. The two African men accompanying him drank Mukaka, a fermented drink made from the same meal, and he had a cool Castle beer.

They set off an hour later taking the branch off the Mutare road the only traffic they would meet now would come from the station some forty kilometres distant. They had gone roughly halfway suddenly the earth erupted on the driver's side as the big machine rose and thumped back to the road, coming to rest at an angle.

"Mine," Angus shouted. The machines were built to

protect its occupants, it had done its job, but it was listing down on one side at the front. He made his way into the rear. The African who had been up on top with the machine gun lay on the floor. Angus crouched beside him to check him out. He was breathing, but bleeding from the mouth.

As he touched the man's shoulder, his eyes opened, and he sat up, wiping the blood from his swollen lips. He spat out two front teeth. The stock of the gun had hit him in the mouth when the vehicle bucked and knocked him out. The driver was in the back now as well.

"What weapons do you have?" Angus asked.

The driver held his hands out, palm up, "Only the big gun on top." he drew a deep breath "What? No rifles" the driver shook his head. "Fuck, we're about twenty kilometres from the station, and this is all we have?"

He pulled his Glock 9-millimetre pistol from its holster and waved it at them.

He climbed out of the back and made his way to the front. The vehicle was going nowhere; the explosion had blown away the suspension. They were going to have to finish the journey on foot; he reckoned it was about twenty kilometres if they stuck to the road, but they could cut five off their journey if they went cross county. He told the African with the injury to wash his mouth out well, it out well until there was no blood in his spit and led them off the road. He didn't want any animals picking up that scent.

Angus moved slowly through the bush stopping every few meters, to study their surroundings, his eyes scanning for any animals, or spoor. The last thing they needed was to come across and pack of Hyenas or Loins armed only with a 9-millimetre pistol.

His shirt front and armpits were darkened with sweat, his hair stuck to his head, and he cursed the fact he hadn't brought a hat when they had left the station.

After a kilometre he signalled them to stop by holding up his fist. A group of Sykes monkeys sat watching them from the branches in a small cluster of Jacaranda trees. He moved in a wide arc around the Jacaranda trees so the monkeys wouldn't raise an alarm call, which could attract other beasts.

They had gone about seven kilometres when the sun had ebbed in the sky. He signalled them to stop again he bent down to look at spoor on the ground. It was still damp; it was leopards spoor and less than an hour old. He knew would still struggle to bring down a lone leopard with a 9-millimetre gun. He reached down and drew the skein-duh from its sheath in his boot with his left hand. The twenty-five-centimetre, double edged blade shone in the failing light. He knew they had to reach the station before dark or they would have to find a suitable Acacia tree to climb and wait the night out.

He pushed on, still fully alert and came to the road where it headed straight to the station. At one point, five kilometres from home, they started to run at a trot.

They covered the distance in twelve minutes. The gates were locked up for the night, but fortunately Manodno had been expecting Angus. When he had seen them coming, he ran to open the gates. When the gates were locked safely behind them, they went to the stoep.

Everyone gathered to welcome Angus back. He told them there was no time for celebration, "Did you know there was major fighting last night at Mutare?" they all looked alarmed and shook their heads.

"We've heard nothing and seen nothing since you went," Lindani told him.

Anashe brought iced tea for the two men he had brought in with him and Castle beer for him. Angus told them the news about Annika and said he would only stay until the replacement warden came, then he would go back to Salisbury.

As others had gone, Anashe was the only woman left on the station now; she brought dinner from the kitchen roast chicken, mashed sweet potato and bread dinner finished as darkness cloaked the station.

Angus told Mandala and Manodno to take the two department men with them to the workshop they could bed down there and reminded them there had to be one man on watch all night, as they left the stoop. He sat with Lindani and Anashe and told them what the doctors had told him and Annika again and said she wouldn't be coming back to Nyanga.

He then told them about the house he had rented and suggested they could come and live with them until they got a house of their own when they came to Salisbury. Angus told Anashe that he would pay her to help Annika with the babies.

"You keep saying babies," Lindani said.

"Oh, I forgot to tell you it was twins. He had only told them Annika would have to stay in the hospital until the birth.

Angus went to the gun cabinet and strapped on a shoulder holster with a Colt Python 1911 .45 pistol in it. After his experience earlier in the day, he was not going to have to depend on his nine-millimetre pistol alone again. Powerful as it was, he thought of it more than a town weapon. He reached at the back of the bottom shelf in the safe and took out the Kudu hide wallet that contained all their paperwork and passports.

Then the box with jewellery he took the necklace and earrings out on the box, put them in his shirt pocket, and buttoned down the flap.

After this he made his way to the office and picked up the

radio microphone. "Nyanga calling station over." When there was no answer, he tried again. There was still no reply. When he was met with silence, he felt relieved at the third attempt when a voice came from the speaker.

"Receiving over." It was Jack Jones at the police station.

"Could you call our department tomorrow and let them know we lost the Crocodile on a landmine? I blew the front suspension off, but we got to our station on foot. Over." He was about to give him the position of the vehicle when Jack answered him again.

"Sorry, we can't do that, Angus. The line is down. The entire area is infested with insurgents. Hundreds have come over the border. Over."

Angus switched the lever again to speak. "What about the army? Over," and threw the lever again to listen.

"They're stretched to breaking point. They've been flying in reserves all day, and the vampire jets have been bombing and strafing the insurgents' current position. It's mayhem. Over."

"Really? It's that bad? Over."

"Yes, you had better keep you guard up. They mean business this time. Where there have been small groups in the past, they're in groups of fifty or more now. Over."

Angus thanked him and called to Lindani. When Lindani arrived in the office Angus was speaking into microphone.

"Manodno bring all the men over here, out."

As soon as they were all present, he began barking orders. "Manodno you and Mandala stay alert tonight. Thank God they haven't come to collect the Crocodile yet. If anything starts and gets too much, we will bring the crocodile over to the workshop, and the four of you be ready to get on board quickly. They all nodded. "Right back to your stations and keep your radio on."

Once they had gone back to the workshop, he told

Lindani to back the crocodile up as close as he could get it to the stoop stairs. When he had done it, Lindani came back.

Angus frowned when he looked at him. "You'll man the cannons, Anashe will sleep in the back. Get plenty of water to see us through. I'll take the roof space. Keep the radio on," he said, as he climbed into the roof space.

Moving from one observation to point to another, Angus scanned the night through the star lit scope. It barely gave him an image as the low cloud obscured the full moon. Then, as if he prayed for it, the cloud broke. He could see to the edge of the vegetation from every vantage point without the scope, but still he moved around in the roof space. He scanned from the back of the house to the front just after midnight.

"Shit" he said and lifted his radio. "Contacts coming from the east." Dropping the radio, he started firing the RPD. There were a lot of them, too many. Lindani and the others joined in with fire power. As he changed magazines, there came a flash from the elephant grass, and he saw the projectile streak its way to the workshop.

It hit and the bright orange explosion sent the roof sheets and timber skywards, then a second struck the workshop an instant later, Angus dropped from the roof space and ran to the Crocodile. Anashe sat on a seat to one side, the two ridgeback dogs at her feet.

"Drive," he barked to Lindani as he swapped places and took over the twin Brownings. The big engine roared into life. Angus wasn't aiming the guns at anything in particular, just spraying the area; the huge weapons spat their deadly load with every fourth round being a tracer round. These streaked bright red as they cut through the night.

As the big machine gathered speed across the compound it smashed through the gates knocking them off their hinges sending them in to the night. He was now firing to the left of the vehicle along the line of insurgents, he saw the flash and instinctively ducks into the truck. An instant later the projectile struck their vehicle with a deafening clatter as it made impact with the upward slopped side of the Crocodile deflecting the force of the explosion skyward.

Angus's heartbeat raced as adrenaline coursed through him, but he kept on firing. Suddenly the guns stopped. There was no more of ammunition; he had fired a thousand rounds. He shouted to Anashe to pass up another two boxes, and he threaded the belts into the breeches of both guns and pulled back both firing blocks.

Lindani drove with the headlights on full beam. The red earth of the road looked even more vivid. Anashe came and touched his boot, signalling him to come down. He dropped into the truck and went to Lindani.

"They're attacking Rusape, they're on the radio asking for help."

The disabled crocodile from the day before loomed into the headlights. Lying half across the dirt road, Lindani slowed to pass it, as the rear sections of the two trucks drew level. Their vehicle suddenly bucked, and the night sky turned orange. Their Crocodile lurched to the left and drooped at the rear. The front single tyre had missed the mine, but the back twin tyres had found it. He jumped down in the available light and saw that the back axle had been mangled, the red road was black where the water used to inflate the tyre instead of air had spilled.

"Fuck...fuck...fuck" Angus said kicking at the still smoking scorched earth. They took what they needed from the truck and disabled the guns by removing the cocking bolts from the twin guns. He threw them in different directions into the bush, then as an afterthought climbed into the other one and did the same.

He had broken his own cardinal rule: he had left his R1 in

the roof space in his haste to get to the Crocodile. He asked Lindani where he was and told him he had left it on the stoep when he was manning the guns on the Crocodile.

"So, all we have are these?" he drew the nine millimetre and pointed to the Colt in his shoulder holster. They couldn't continue on the road as Rusape was under attack. "What will we do now?" he asked Lindani.

"We should go through the bush. We have less chance of being found." Angus nodded. But he felt scared at the prospect of walk through the bush with so little protection and having Aneshe with them. She would slow them down.

"How long will that take us to get to Salisbury, it's a hundred and fifty kilometres," Lindani told him he had walked with his father went he was young. It had taken them two days. They left the road with Lindani in the lead, the two dogs and Anashe behind him, and Angus followed at the rear. Thankfully, now that the clouds had cleared, they had bright moonlight. The sounds of the African night filled the air as they walked.

As they headed west crickets fell silent as they approached them, then continued their noise when they passed. A lion somewhere in the distance grunted. As the moon waned in the west, the sky changed to gold behind them. By then, they had covered ten kilometres.

They rested and Lindani went to a cactus plant, gathered a hand full of grass and cut some prickly pears. The round orange pears were coated in very fine spikes that were hard to remove if they got on the skin. He brought them to where Anashe was, and he waited.

Angus drew his Skean Dhu from his boot and handed it to Lindani, as he had watched him peel the fruits many times before. He pierced some fruit with the pointed dagger and skinned it with his skinning knife. The orange flesh tasted of melon.

As the sun reached its peak, they were twenty-five kilometres closer to Salisbury. The heat was oppressive heat when Lindani pointed to a Jacaranda tree bathed in hot purple flowers. "We will rest there until the shadows grow," he said. Once under the shade, Lindani told Angus and Anashe to wait. Their mouths were dry as the juice from the prickly pears had long since worn off and the heat was draining them.

As Angus sat in shadows, he watched a paradise flycatcher warbling as he hopped from branch to branch of a Bilbao tree, showing off his long orange breeding tail as he tried to attract a mate.

Lindani had not been gone long when he came back carrying three Narra melons.

Their yellow horned skins split to reveal the green juicy meat. They loosened them with the skinning knife and scooped it with their fingers. It tasted of cucumber and lemon but was enough to bring moisture to their dry mouths. They started out again as the savannah stretched out before them. The trees and termite mounds shimmered through the heat haze, but that was about to change. The sky in the distance was dark and lightning bolts streaked earthwards. As it came closer the black clouds seemed to touch the ground and the rumble of thunder became sudden claps directly above them as torrential rain fell. "We must find cover," Lindani said.

It was never good to be caught in the savannah. In fierce storms the lightning bolts bounced from rock to rock and was it was deadly. The rain fell so heavily it cut their vision to thirty meters.

When they came to a large Acacia tree more by luck than navigational skill, the umbrella of dense foliage offered them some protection from the rain. That day they knew they would get no further; they spent the night there, a miserably cold night while the rain had been refreshing in the day's heat. Now they shivered as the wet clothes clung to them.

Thankfully, as dawn's light edged in the rain finally stopped, heralding in a bleak day. The skies were still heavy with cloud, but it quickened their pace to shake the chill from their bodies.

CHAPTER 27

A telephone rang on Ted Hibbins desk. The call came from the department's transport section. The transport that went to Nyanga had failed to return. He telephoned Brady barracks to ask if he could find out anything. All they could tell him was the whole eastern highlands area was under intense pressure from insurgents. He tried to call the Nyanga police post, but the line was dead, and Ted immediately felt alarmed that he had Angus to his death.

What am I going to tell Annika? How can I face her?

Late afternoon a call came from Brady barracks, a helicopter had flown over Nyanga station on its way to refuel, one building had been destroyed, and there were bodies on the ground.

The little bell rang at seven o'clock, and Ted's heart filled with dread as he walked through the ward doors, solemn faced.

Annika smiled when she saw him. "Nice to see you, Ted," but when he didn't return her smile, his haunted expression told her something was wrong. "What is it Ted, what's wrong?"

He sat on the chair beside her bed and took her hand. He did not know how to tell her what he knew. "I don't know how to say this, Annika, but something has happened at Nyanga."

Her face paled. "What? What's happened?"

He shrugged and squeezed her hand. "I don't know. A helicopter reported the station had been attacked and one of the buildings had been destroyed."

Annika shook, and tears pricked her eyes. "Angus... what about Angus?" "No word, I only know what the guy from the barracks said."

Tears streamed down her cheeks. "Are you upsetting my patient?"

He looked up at the matron, "Sorry we've got a bit of uncertain news," he told her.

Annika's face reddened, and she lurched forward, clutching her stomach, beads of sweat showing on her forehead. The matron drew the curtain around the bed and took her wrist, looking at the watch she had pinned on her uniform.

When she finished, she told Ted he had to leave, and that she was calling for the doctor. "I think she's going into premature labour. Ted stood, kissed her on the forehead. "Sorry, I'll be back as soon as I've got anything else to tell you," he said and left.

* * *

THEY WERE LOOKING for a suitable place to spend the night as the light faded when Lindani held his hand up and whispered. "Hyenas".

When they got closer Angus heard the whoop, whoop noise they made as came in to sight; he counted fifteen in the clan laughing.

Heads drooping with bared toothed slavering smiles, he handed Lindani the 9-millimetre pistol, drew his colt and pulled the cocking slide back.

Lindani pointed to a big Bilbao "Get up in that tree but move slowly. The hyenas got bolder, and the two ridgebacks growled, showing their teeth, but even they knew they would be no match for so many hyenas. Suddenly one of them made to charge.

Lindani took aim and pulled the trigger even with one hand holding his shooting wrist, the big pistol jumped. He hit the beast behind its left shoulder, rib bone and blood exploded from the beast's right side, as the impact knocked it sideways, and it fell.

The other hyenas retreated, startled by the noise of the gun. As they headed for the tree slowly, the hyenas started tearing at their hunting companion, squabbling noisily. Darkness fell as they climbed into the branches of the big Bilbao tree. "What about the dogs?" Angus asked.

"They will look after themselves. They could run all night if they have to, the hyenas are too slow for them," Lindani said.

The clan milled around the bottom of the tree, trying every now and again to reach up the trunk, looking up with bloodied muzzles, then eventually gave up and wandered away into the night.

A light persistent rain fell though out the night after the main body of another storm passed, soaking them again. It was a second night with little or no sleep. As the skies lightened, the clouds had passed and the sky glowed orange in the east. The weather was going to go from one extreme to the other.

The sun rose over the horizon. As its rays fell on the savannah, the wet vegetation gave off a heavy mist. All they could see was the upper branches of trees in a white calm sea. They climbed down from the sanctuary of their perch, steam rose from their clothes and bodies. Lindani let out a whistle and seconds later the two ridgeback dogs came out of the mist. He patted both.

"I will go and find food," he said. They had not eaten since the prickly pears and bush melon.

"You and Anashe head west, I will find you."

They had gone about two kilometres further on when he rejoined them. The sun was burning the mist from the savannah and visibility on the ground was better. He had brought some mangos and oranges, which weren't ripe and tasted very bitter, but the juice was energy and liquid.

Again, when the sun reached high in the sky, it was another hot oppressive day. They rested under the shade of a small group of Pompom trees, In the shade, the pink globular flower heads gave off their sweet scent, but even in the shade the heat made Angus feel nauseas. When Lindani went foraging again; Angus sat with his knees up, head resting on folded arms, and drifted in and out of sleep.

He woke with a start when Lindani came back and stood before him. He had pockets full of olives and carried bunches of Lanbai grapes. The grapes were delicious and quenched their thirsts. They rested until the sun was midway between late afternoon and sunset and set off again. When the bush grew thicker, they stuck to game tracks to change direction from time to time. The brush cleared as they reached the edge of a Tabaco plantation, the shoulder high manicured rows of plants stretched in the distance.

Lindani pointed to the north, "The farm is in that direction, maybe a one-hour walk."

Angus nodded. "Okay, we'll make for that."

They made excellent progress as the red earth was clear between the rows of foliage. When the farm building came into view, relief flooded Angus's body. A rumble of thunder rolled over the savannah. They approached the edge of the fence with caution.

"Hello in the farm."

"Who's there?" came a reply.

"We are from Nyanga game station."

They waited a moment before he heard, "Come on in."

A small man in front of the house greeted them. He was a small overweight man. He didn't look much like how a farmer should, and his paunch was supported by a broad brass buckled belt. Attached to the belt was a holster with a big revolver in it; he wore it cowboy style. Angus almost chuckled when he thought the man reminded him of the little fat guy in the John Wayne film he saw with Morag.

Angus held out his hand and introduced himself. He took his hand.

"Hendrick Balling," he replied. He directed them onto the house stoop. A woman came from the house door. "My wife, Sahara," he announced as he held out an upturned hand. She was a slim woman in her fifties with a shock of red hair and ice-blue eyes. She stood a good fifty centimetres taller than her husband.

They all shook her hand Angus imagined she must have been a good-looking woman in her younger days, as he shook her hand.

"I don't suppose you have a telephone?"

"We do, but it's been out of order for the past three days."

"Have you got a radio?"

The farmer shook his head, "We've never needed one."

The storm was now in full swing thunder clapped overhead and it seemed to shake the building; lightning flashed, turning the sheets of rain sliver. They ate at a big kitchen table as the wind whipped at the house, rattling the doors, and crashing the rain into the panes of glass in the windows.

Hendrick agreed to have one of his men drive them the seventy-five kilometres to Salisbury the next morning.

* * *

THE SWEAT GLISTENED on her face as she strained under the bright surgical light. The veins strained on Annika's neck and wrists, as her nails dug into the palms of her hands. The matron mopped her brow with a cold compress, as the midwife watched the progress of the birth under the sheet draped over her raised legs supported by stirrups.

She had been taken to the delivery room three times since Hibbard's visit, each time only to be taken back to the main ward as the pains of labour wore off and no progress was being made.

After her last visit to the labour ward, the doctor examined her and asked if she wanted a caesarean section. Annika asked if it was necessary. When he told her it wasn't, she continued to try to have the babies naturally. She put the gas and air mask back to her mouth as another bout of pain wracked her body.

"Okay, a big push this time," the midwife ordered. Annika strained her face turned deep red, almost purple. "Okay," the midwife said, "the rest of first baby's head is out." Annika panted and took another gulp from the mask. "Right Annika, one last push, you can do it." She did with a grunt, "Excellent," the midwife said from behind the sheet. "Hello little man," she said as she cut the cord and passed the baby to the waiting nurse.

"It's a boy?" Annika said, smiling, but looking exhausted.

"Yes, now come on, this is nearly over. I need you to do the same again." Annika sucked on the mask again and strained. She didn't get time to rest. "Well done, the head has crowned. Two more pushes and the second baby came out.

"Come and meet your brother" the midwife said, "it's another boy."

A short time later they brought the two babies to her. She cried as she looked down at them on either arm. Joy mixed with an overwhelming feeling of loss and helplessness, wondering what happened to Angus.

* * *

THE VISITOR'S bell woke Annika. When she opened her eyes, the screen was drawn around her bed. She could hear the other patient's visitors, but no one came for her. Eventually, she drifted off to sleep again.

Later she lay awake in the semidarkness, the only light in the ward coming from the night light on the nurse's desk at the other end of the ward. Annika began to cry. She had a family, but did she still have a husband, or had she lost a second one to Africa? She never slept again that night, even although she was exhausted. They had brought her babies for her to feed and taken them back to the nursery.

* * *

ANGUS HAD A SENSE OF EUPHORIA. Was it the feeling of relief from being out of the bush? Or the excitement that he would see Annika again?

He sat on the stoep when the storm had passed, the fragrance of the foliage surrounding the farm filled the air. As he sat, he looked to the heavens, the kaleidoscope of stars filled the sky, reminding him of Scotland on one of the clear nights in winter.

One of the farm hands came and asked him if he wanted tea or coffee.

"Tea." he said. *When was the last time I drank tea?*

The night sky waned as the light crept in, and the stars began to fade as Lindani and Anashe came across from the building that accommodated the farm hands. After breakfast they thanked Hendrick and Sahara for their help and hospitality and told them they would have the Toyota they were to travel in re-fuelled before it returned.

They waved from the back of the pickup truck as they left, Anashe travelled inside with the two farm hands, while Lindani and Angus travelled on the rear with the two dogs.

Two hours passed and Angus gave the driver directions to the hospital when they came in to the city.

As he jumped from the back of the truck, he told Lindani to take them to the department offices and arrange the re-fuelling for them, and to contact Ted Hibbins and tell him to put fifty dollars in an envelope and give it to the driver to be taken back to Hendrick."

Annika sat on the chair next to her bed when she heard the commotion outside the ward door.

The matron, not the same one with the bell, was refusing Angus entry. He pushed past her and opened the door.

"Annika!" she took a deep gasp when she saw him.

"Angus, you're alive," the anguish in her tone made Angus's chest tighten. She stood up as he reached her taking her in an embrace and kissed her passionately to some other patients' amusement.

He let her go as if in shock and looked down at her stomach. It wasn't flat, but much smaller than it had been when he left.

"The babies? What happened to the babies?"

She smiled. "We have two sons, Angus."

Tears immediately rolled down his cheeks as he embraced her again.

A hand fell on his shoulder. "You can't bring that in here." He spun around to face the matron.

"Bring what in?"

She pointed the Colt on his ribs. He told her he had come straight from the bush; she said she knew this, but couldn't allow him to stay because he was armed. Angus took off the gun and took dismantled it.

"Better?"

"She picked up the bullets and the barrel and stuffed them in her uniform pocket. "Now," she smiled. "Come and meet your boys."

Both babies were asleep in cots, side by side, in the nursery. He touched each of their faces. "They are beautiful, Annika, thank you."

She smiled "I couldn't have done it without you." She winked and his face reddened as the matron smiled. He spent an hour with her in a common room away from the ward; he took the kudu hide wallet from inside his shirt.

"I've got all our papers," he said as he laid it on a small table.

"What about the jewellery? she asked. Unbuttoning his shirt pocket, he took them out and handed them to her. "They still look beautiful." she said. As an afterthought, he brought the Rolex from his other pocket and slipped it on his wrist.

The matron came and told him he would have to go as the doctor was on his rounds; he asked her how long they would keep her in hospital, and she told him she would ask the doctor.

When Angus walked into the morning sun, Lindani and Anashe were sitting on a bench in the hospital gardens.

"How is Annika? Lindani asked.

Angus punched the air. "We have twin boys." Passers-by turned and look at him.

Lindani grinned. "And Annika?"

"She's fine." he said, "we're all fine."

"Come," Angus said. "We'll get a cab to the bank, then go to your new home."

"No need Ted told me to give you these," Lindani threw Angus his car keys and nodded toward the Chrysler. The dogs' heads were hanging out the rear windows.

They all went visiting that night and the matron relaxed her rule of two to a bed, She even allowed them all to see the babies at once.

He asked when they could take them home; she smiled for the first time since he had encountered her. "They're small but a good weight and doing well. They are feeding so they can go home tomorrow, after the doctor does his rounds."

* * *

AFTER THE PREVIOUS couple of days, they slept late into the morning. When they took the short drive in to the city, he stopped at the bank again and withdrew a thousand dollars.

All three of them spent the day baby shopping, with Anashe picking out everything necessary for two new babies. Angus paid for two of everything: cots, clothes, feeding bottles the list was endless. Before he went to the hospital, he dropped Landani at the house with all the shopping.

When Angus pulled up in the hospital car park and lifted the big box of chocolates from the passenger seat, it wasn't something he'd thought of, but Annika had told him to get them for the staff as a thank you.

He looked at the time on his Rolex, four o'clock. When he went up to the ward door, a nurse told him the doctor was on the ward and he would have to wait.

Annika appeared at the ward door; she was dressed to leave in her now baggy clothes she had worn when he had taken her in.

Angus settled his wife in the back seat of the Chrysler. The two nurses who carried the babies to the car passed one to Annika, and the other to Anashe. The babies behaved well on their first journey home. Lindani was pacing the garden as Angus pulled into the driveway and ran around opening the doors for everyone.

Once they all had held each baby in turn, they settled them in their cots, Lindani had put up, then they all sat in the garden at the rear at Annika's request. She had not been in the open air for nearly two weeks. Lindani and Anashe ate and went to bed, leaving them alone.

"What are we going to call the babies" she asked.

Angus shrugged. "You pick the names," he said. She thought for a moment. "Angus,"

"What?" He asked.

She chuckled. "We'll call our first born, Angus."

He nodded with a lump in his throat, touched she wanted to name their first son named after him. "Now you must choose for the other one," she told him.

"Yannie," he said, "we will call the other one Yannie… if that's okay with you?"

Tears pricked her eyes, and she gave him a sad smile. "I would like that."

Next day they told Lindani and Anashe the names they had chosen, Lindani asked which one is Angus as they stood beside the cots. They both shrugged. They were identical twins, and only Annika could tell them apart. "Okay," Annika said, "This one is Angus, and this one Yannie."

Lindani and Anesh left Annika and Angus at home with the twins and went shopping for the list Annika gave them. They sat again in the garden under the shade of a parasol. "Angus?"

"What" she looked apprehensive. "I don't want our babies to live here in Africa."

Angus looked stunned and said nothing. "Africa has cost us both too many losses." They fell quiet, each thinking their own thoughts.

"What's brought this on?" Angus eventually asked.

She drew a breath. "I made my mind up in hospital, I thought I had lost you."

"But I'm safe, Annika." she shook her head. "Not only has Africa cost me one husband, and you a wife, we have lost our home in Nyanga. I won't let it take anything else from me." Tears streaked down her face and Angus's heart broke to see her this way.

"Okay," he agreed. "but we will wait until the boys are a little older before we travel." The look of relief on Annika's face said it all.

A taxi pulled up at the gate as the sun was going down Ted gave him a wave as he sat on the stoep; he was carrying two enormous blue teddy bears.

"Come to see the young'uns," he said.

He went through the usual routine of which of the babies was which, and how was Annika feeling. Angus had been on his third beer with Angus as they sat alone at the back of the house. Lindani and Anashe had gone to the cinema, and Annika had gone to bed after feeding the twins.

"Ted, we have something to tell you. We won't be coming back to work with the department."

"Oh, why not?"

"We are leaving Africa. Annika doesn't want to take the chance of bringing our sons up here."

He considered what Angus told him and nodded. "So where are you going to go?"

"Anywhere but Africa," Annika told him, appearing at the back door.

They broke the news to Lindani and Anashe the next morning, but assured them they would make sure they were settled before they went. Angus went to see Ted and asked him where they were going to house Lindani and Anashe. He told him they were to look for a place to rent for them when he and Annika left.

"What about our house?" Angus suggested.

"How much is the rent?"

"one fifty a month."

"that's little too high," he said.

"What's the upper limit?" Angus asked.

He thought for a moment "Say one twenty."

Angus told him to leave it with him and he drove straight over to Brady barracks.

He asked the guard on the gate if he could see Mrs Renshaw and was told to wait. A few minutes later he saw her walk across the parade ground. She was in uniform and a sergeant. "Is there a problem?" she asked. Her voice seemed somehow different now she was in uniform.

Angus he told her they would give up the house. "I can't give you your money back, I'm afraid." She told him she had been in arrears with the mortgage.

"What time are you off duty?" he asked.

"Four o'clock."

"Would you like to have dinner with my wife and I at the house?" She considered for a moment and smiled. "Yes, I'd like that."

He told her they would eat at seven thirty. As he walked to his car, he heard his name being called. Jim McGovern hobbled toward him on crutches. His right leg was heavily bandaged.

"What the hell happened to you?" Angus asked.

"Fucking mine. My partner stood on it and I caught some shrapnel."

"Are you going to be okay?"

He shrugged. "Doc says he had to remove a lot of damaged calf muscle."

Angus told him about the twins and was congratulated once more.

"What are you going to do now?"

McGovern gestured at his leg. "Christ alone knows if they throw me out. I would be on a plane back to the UK, if I had the money," and shook his head.

"How would you like to come to dinner tonight?" McGovern's face brightened.

"Love to."

"Ok seven thirty Oh! And there is another squaddie is coming. Jan Renshaw, ask if she can drive you up."

McGovern winked and smiled "she will."

He made two stops on his way home; one to the butcher shop he had bought the supplies he'd taken to Nyanga and bought a fillet of beef and six potted hocks. He told Annika what was said at his meeting with Ted, and that he had invited the house owner and McGovern to dinner.

He told her he was going to ask Jan Renshaw if she would lower the rent, so that when they left Lindani and Anashe could stay on at the house.

Dinner was ready when Angus saw the headlights shine on the lounge window as it swung into the driveway. He went to greet them, Jan first, then McGovern, as he hobbled behind her. He introduced Jan Renshaw to Annika then Lindani then Anashe, and then McGovern asked to see the twins.

When he broached the subject after about the rent after dinner, Jan told him she couldn't afford to drop it, as she had to pay rent herself at the barracks.

That's why she had got into arrears with the mortgage, when the house was empty. As the women talked about babies, Angus said to McGovern, "Want a breath of fresh air?"

They went into garden it was a balmy night with a full moon, the smell of jasmine filled the air. Angus stopped walking "Here," he said, and gave him an envelope. "What's this?

"Look and see."

McGovern opened it and took out the contents. "What the hell is this?"

They're for you and Sandy Ewan," he told him. He had bought them on the second stop on his way home. two one way tickets from Johannesburg to Heathrow, and two from Heathrow to Glasgow. "We canny take these aff ye man, they must hiv cost ye a bundle. Ye'v goat weans noo."

Angus laughed. "Practicing your Glaswegian already? They're yours for the second of next month, so try not to get yourself killed between now and then."

He looked at the tickets again. "I'll pay you back for these, Angus."

He shook his head then added, "Well if you're ever that flush, stick some money in an envelope and send it to my father."

The guests left at ten o'clock, Jan explained she was on duty at six the next morning. Angus explained to Lindani what Ted, and he had discussed that morning. But would go back and see him again in the morning and see if he could find a way around the house rent.

When they were alone, Annika asked him where they should go when they left.

"It's up to you," she shook her head.

"No, Angus, this must be a joint decision."

They sat and thought. "I would prefer Europe," she said.

"Okay, but where?"

She took his hand and clasped their fingers together. "We have enough money. I could start my own practice."

Angus agreed and nodded, "But where?"

"Well, I am a vet and you said there are plenty of sheep and cattle in Scotland no?"

The decision came as a shock to him. "Are you sure?"

She shrugged. "From what I hear property is very expensive in the Netherlands."

He looked at her. "How do you know this? You have been away for years."

"Carine Laroy had newspapers her sister had sent her from home. I read them from start to finish when I was bored."

* * *

ONE MONTH LATER ANGUS, Annika and their children left Rhodesia. Ted Hibbins had given Lindani a pay rise to compensate for the rent, and Angus gave the couple the Chrysler and his Sgian-Dubh. They had all lost dear friends Manodno and Mandala in the explosion in the workship, at Nyanga Wildlife station.

Customs at Jan Smuts Airport took them aside when they had filled out the declaration papers regarding what they were taking out of South Africa.

He silently thanked John Green for the receipt he had given them with the valuable diamond necklace and earrings.

They sat in the departure lounge, each nursing one of their boys when they spotted two familiar faces: Jim McGovern and Sandy Ewan.

The Boeing 747 roared down the runway at Jan Smuts airport and climbed into the blue sky, circling Johannesburg beneath it as it sought out its flightpath. On the plane sat Angus and Annika McLean, holding a baby boy each in their arms. The boys were both gaining height. A wave of relief washed over Angus's wife as she stared out the window at hazy scene below. She wasn't sad to be leaving the country behind, and whispered, "Sorry, I couldn't allow you to take anything else from me, Africa."

ABOUT THE AUTHOR

Jamie Scott is an emerging author of action adventure fiction.

Being a Scot living in South Africa around the time for the Rhodesian Bush War, Jamie's first novel is a work of fiction based loosely on memories and representation of some characters he met, who had lived the nightmare of the Bush War. Good men he feels he had the good fortune and pleasure of spending time with there.

Printed in Great Britain
by Amazon

59626235R00149